SUCKER FOR A SIREN

FOLK HAVEN BOOK TWO

LAUREN CONNOLLY

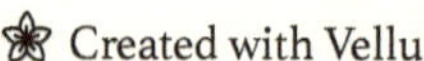 Created with Vellum

ACKNOWLEDGMENTS

Thank you to Kenzie and Katy for your beta-reading insights. You helped me solve the puzzles I hadn't known I had.

Thank you, Jovana, for your editing expertise and enthusiasm for Folk Haven. My books would be a sloppy mess without your skilled eye and insightful comments.

And as always, this series would never have had the time and space to grow if it wasn't for my supportive and loving parents. Mom and Dad, you don't know how much it means to me that I can ramble to you both about romance writing for an entire dinner and not have you searching for a way to escape!

CONTENT WARNING

This book contains scenes with choking, violence, and unhealthy parental relationships as well as discussions of captivity, abuse, manipulative relationships, and sexual assault.

1

—————

SEAMUS

I THOUGHT I would have more time to prepare. When I step into Coffee & Claws, I expect to see a long line. A bunch of people strung out between me and the counter, acting as a slow interlude to the ordering process. A brief buffer between me and her.

But there's nothing in my way. No pause I can take other than standing here, just inside the door, awkwardly staring around, as if confused as to why I came to this coffee shop.

I came to order tea. Tea I could easily brew for myself at home.

But she's not at my house.

Neri.

The woman prominent in my mind stands behind the counter, her back to me as she converses with whoever is working in the kitchen. At least that inattention provides me a moment to readjust. To try imbuing confidence in my stride as I approach the register. And her.

My eyes fix on the swing of Neri's ponytail as she gives a

nod. The white-blonde hair, lighter even than her pale skin, has a little swoop in it. A bend I want to follow by sliding the band out and combing my fingers through the strands.

Neri faces me, and my gut tightens. Her smile is soft, but those silvery eyes are sharp, taking in every inch of me. "Hi, Seamus. Earl Grey? Or you wanna go wild today and get hibiscus?"

The sound of my name in her melodious voice flows along my nerve endings. I shouldn't get too excited about her knowing it. She's written it on a cup every day for the past three weeks.

Because, yeah, I've been pining after her that long. Coming back to this coffee shop just to bask in her attention for the time it takes to place my order.

"Hello, Neri." I take pride in how casual I sound. As if I didn't look forward to the single moment I got to say her name every day. "It appears I'm going to be boring today."

"Oh well. I'll convince you one of these days." She grabs the twenty-ounce cup because if I'm going to buy my tea from this shop, I'm at least going to get a large dose.

Normally, Neri writes my name in quick, neat letters, moving on from me so she can get to the next customer. But there's no one behind me in the line, and maybe that's why the slate-eyed woman of my fantasies takes her time, drawing the *S* of my name so it covers a good portion of the cup.

This is my chance. Time to move past the same small talk we exchange every time I come here. Why didn't I prepare any talking points?

"So ... you're a barista." I clear my throat. "That's ... fascinating."

Curse The Finned One's games. What did I just say?

Neri pauses in the middle of writing the *M* to look up at me. Her smile tilts at the corner now, and I focus on the small change. In indication this conversation is not like all the others.

"I guess. Making fancy coffee is a kind of skill set. Quicker to learn than others though. But it has given me some calluses." She places the marker on the counter and extends her arm, holding her palm up for me to see.

With that offering, I can't help leaning in closer, getting a good look at her skin. Every line and crease read as perfection to me. But I do see the calluses along with a fading redness.

"What's that from?" My original question was all fumbling, but true curiosity helps untangle my tongue.

"Steaming the milk." Neri scoops up a little metal container, showing it to me. "I keep my hand wrapped around the side while I'm steaming. When I can barely stand to hold it anymore, that's when I know it's done."

"That's barbaric!" Acting on instinct, I reach out, encircling her wrist with my fingers, brushing a thumb across her poor, abused skin. "Can't you use a thermometer instead?"

When I meet her eyes, something sparks in the gray irises.

"Thermometers are for wimps." She smirks.

The ring of the shop door opening breaks our stare, and Neri pulls her hand from mine. Shocked at the liberty I took, I shove my own hands in my pockets.

"What about a cookie?" Her singsong voice teases over the last word.

"What's that?" I'm having trouble focusing as I try to tattoo the memory of the feel of her on my brain.

"Can I convince you to buy a cookie?" The tempting barista waves at the pastry display case. "They just came out of the oven a few minutes ago. Their insides are probably still soft and warm."

Oh gods. Who would've thought hearing a woman discuss baked goods could turn me on?

I clear my throat and nod. "You choose."

That earns me a wide grin I'm sure is lethal from the erratic effect it has on my heart.

"How about peanut butter?"

"Good." I need this interaction to be over as much as I want to talk to her forever.

Thankfully, Neri slides the treat into a paper sleeve, finishes writing my name on my cup, and rings me up. After I pull my credit card from the machine, her glance slides over my shoulder to where another customer waits.

Dismissed, I head to the other end of the counter, leaning against a high-top table as I wait for her to fill my cup with scalding water and add the bag of Earl Grey. I hope Neri doesn't use her bare hand to tell if the water is hot enough. If I find I'm contributing to the irritation on her palm, I'll have to switch to iced tea.

"I'm heading to the bank." Sonya, one of the owners of Coffee & Claws, strolls out of a back office. She leans over the counter, loose black curls swinging against copper cheeks as she catches Neri's eye. "You and Heath hold down the fort while I'm gone."

"Got it, boss." Neri offers a thumbs-up and another of her stunning grins.

Sonya catches my eye on the way out and smirks. "Hey, Seamus. Back for more tea?"

She knows. Of course she does.

I came in here yesterday and found Sonya at the cash register instead of the employee I wanted to see. When I asked if Neri was working, my attempt to sound nonchalant probably came off as hopeless.

"Yes." *I am not blushing.* "I love tea."

Sonya's chuckle lingers, even after she leaves the shop.

Pushing the woman's reaction from my mind, I refocus on the present moment. The paper surrounding my cookie crinkles in my hand, warmth seeping through the thin barrier. Did Neri realize what she was saying? What my dirty mind would think with those words hanging in the air between us?

"Their insides are probably still soft and warm."

Stop with the dirty thoughts, I chastise myself. *She was just helping a customer. Not flirting.*

If I want a hope of Neri looking at me in any kind of way, I'll need to ask her out. That's not something I normally balk at. Not since my early twenties. But asking Neri on a date seems infinitely more difficult than starting up the past relationships I've had.

I've only ever dated selkies or humans. As a selkie myself, that's normal. Mythics are expected to date their own kind or a non-mythical being.

But Neri is a siren.

Sonya is Neri's cousin and a siren herself. She let the Town Council know about the new mythic arrival, which isn't required but strongly suggested. My sister, Moira, was the one to tell me Neri's species.

I have nothing against sirens. The problem is cross-mythic dating. Our society frowns on it. Because the children of those couples always come out ... different.

A selkie with a selkie makes a selkie.

A selkie with a human makes a selkie most often, occasionally a human.

A selkie with any other mythic makes a mystery, and that lack of clarity scares people.

But my younger brother Calder just paired up with a dragon named Delta. If he can do it, why can't I?

I'm going to ask her out, I decide. *If she turns me down, well, then I can at least get over this whole pining nonsense. And stop spending so much money on tea.*

I pass my cookie from hand to hand while brainstorming the best way to go about my mission. Should I write my phone number on a card and tell her to call me? Ask her to her face right now? Wait till she gets off work? But that would mean lurking around here, and I've been trying hard not to appear creepy.

As I ponder my problem, I break off a cookie chunk and pop it in my mouth. Then, I almost let out a curse because, damn, this pastry is good. Sweet and salty and nutty. Warm and soft, just like Neri promised. My next piece is even larger, and I shove the chunk in my mouth when I hear her voice again.

"Seamus. Your tea."

So lost in my head, I draw in a surprised breath at the sound of Neri's humming voice caressing my name. Unfortunately, my gasp ends up sucking a good portion of the cookie down my esophagus. My air supply immediately dwindles, and I begin to panic, trying to cough but unable to catch the breath needed to expel the object from my lungs.

Stars burst in the corners of my eyes, and sweat breaks out all over my body as my temperature rises with panic. Someone shouts nearby, but I'm too busy trying to get my brain to save me to hear the words. I can solve this problem if only I can think, but adrenaline flashes a strobe light in my mind.

Hard, abrupt pressure hits my stomach, and I let out a pathetic wheeze. There's another slam of something against my solar plexus, forcing the air in my lungs to shove out the cookie chunk, and finally, I can breathe again.

Coughing up crumbs and spit, I collapse into a chair and focus on pulling in breath after breath. Sweet oxygen, more delicious than any baked good.

Eventually, the world around me clarifies, and I notice a reassuring loop getting traced along my back. Someone's flat hand eases the tension in my spine with their thoughtful strokes.

"How are you doing?" Neri asks. "Want a glass of water?"

I glance up then and find the siren hovering over me. Her hand is the one working calming circles. Then, pausing her stroking and moving slowly, Neri cups my face in her palms.

Her worried gray eyes stare into mine, her warm skin glorious on my cheeks.

Neri is the reason I can breathe again.

She saved me.

The sharp spike of gratitude sinks away, replaced by horror.

Neri saved my life. She rescued me when I was in danger, which, in selkie legends, means one thing.

The gods do not control me! a voice howls in my head. *I am in control of my life! There is no fate!*

"Seamus?"

I launch up from the chair, away from the siren's intoxicating comfort, and glare at her.

"You are *not* my mate!"

2

———

NERI

GOING through a near-death experience can cause people to act strange, but I wasn't expecting what amounts to the opposite of a marriage proposal.

"Excuse me?"

Seamus backs away from me like I'm brandishing a knife at him.

"I am *not* your mate. So, don't even think it."

What in the name of The Winged One?

A moment ago, this guy was the perfect combination of cute and sexy. Every time Seamus comes into the shop, I stand taller and smile brighter, all from the anticipation of getting to exchange a few words with him. Today, I even flirted despite the fact I'd put a pause on all relationships for the foreseeable future.

And now, he's yelling at me? About wanting to shack up with him? After I saved his life?

"I wasn't thinking it," I snap at him, crossing my arms over my chest. The arms, I'd like to point out, that I just used to save his life.

"Good. Because it's not happening." His stare stays on me, wary distrust twisting a face I used to think was handsome.

How has his previously adorable, curly hair, falling against snow-pale skin, lost its charm? How have his sharp jaw with its cleft chin and soft brown eyes gotten so ugly in the matter of seconds?

"I don't want it to happen!" *And now, I'm shouting at my job. Great.*

The few people in Coffee & Claws stare between the two of us. I hope they're all as confused as I am.

"Just FYI," I growl, "I'm not on the market. And if I were, I sure as hell wouldn't want to get involved with an ungrateful prick like you!"

Whirling around, I snatch up his cup of tea and then turn back to slam it down on the table between us. I avert my eyes from his name on the side, where I tried to add a few extra flourishes because I was giving in to an irrational sense of giddiness earlier. "Here's your drink, *sir*." From years of practice, I drag on my perky customer-service face. The one that hides a boiling anger just beneath the surface. "Have a *lovely* day."

And then I stride back to the counter, somehow not flipping the asshole off during my exit.

Heath, one of my bosses and a co-owner of the shop, has his salt-and-pepper head poking through the window to the kitchen when I approach. His pale cheeks are ruddy, most likely from the hot oven he bakes all his delicious treats in.

"Wanna take your fifteen?" The bear shifter is a perceptive mythic, likely able to sniff out my fury if he didn't hear my snarling from a moment ago.

"Love to." I toss my apron under the counter and stride down the back hall, exiting through an employees-only door.

Jogging past the dumpster and through a small parking lot, I quickly reach the forest that presses against the edge of the town.

Folk Haven, a lakeside settlement in northern Georgia, is supposed to be my new home. The perfect place for me to get a fresh start among a population with a higher percentage of mythics than anywhere else in the world. Here, surrounded by magical beings, I thought I might finally figure out how to become comfortable with all parts of my identity and use that growth to discover what I want to do with my life.

I imagined Folk Haven as an oasis of support in an otherwise dangerous world.

But being a mythical creature doesn't prevent someone from also being an assface. I'll have to remember that.

I weave through the trees until I find the picnic table Heath showed me on my first day of work. The old, weather-warped wood is soft under my butt as I settle in. But just as I sit down, I'm back up again, angry energy needing to be dispelled.

My shoulder blades itch.

What I wouldn't give to be in an open, secluded space where I could truly let go.

"Sirens don't need to unfurl their wings. They simply want to." My mother's voice sounds clear in my head.

Yeah, well, I didn't *need* to leave my job at their restaurant and move across the country to get away from their expectations.

I simply wanted to.

Running with that logic, I almost strip off my shirt and let my wings out now. But even in Folk Haven, I can't do everything I want, whenever I want. Which would include cursing out that infuriating man who let me think he was a decent guy before flipping his douche-bag switch.

"It's for the better," I grumble to myself.

I just got out of one major dud of a relationship. No need to be searching for another.

Even if I never planned on dating Seamus, I enjoyed watching him approach my counter. Getting a chance to smile at him and ask silly questions. And today, that brief swipe of his thumb across my palm, I *really* enjoyed that.

Innocent flirtations added excitement to my days.

And he ruined it.

With a groan, I settle onto the bench, letting my arms fold on the tabletop and my head collapse onto their pillow. Now, without the distraction of a cute guy buying tea, there's nothing left to stop me from focusing on how directionless my life is.

"You'll take over the family business. We've made everything easy for you." My mother's voice comes again.

Moving across the country from her hasn't stopped her from being my constant companion. A judgmental bird perched on my shoulder, tweeting expectations in my ear.

Yes, my parents paved an easy path for me to follow. Picking everything out in my life for me, arranging my future exactly to their specifications, until I felt like a living doll.

Who knows? Maybe if I hadn't run, they would have eventually started moving my limbs for me too.

Not my wings, of course. If my parents had their choice, those would always stay safely tucked away.

Reaching a hand back, I search under the neck of my shirt and press against the smooth flesh of my upper back. The magic I was born with keeps everything flat and unmarred but for a barely discernible line, like a well-healed scar. At that tease of sensation against my fingertips, I give myself a goal. Something to aim for. One part of my life where I can say I have purpose.

Soon, I will find a safe place to stretch my wings.

3

───────

NERI

"I HEAR you had a run-in with a selkie today."

"Heath told you, didn't he?" I cringe as I set down my wineglass on the kitchen island and turn toward my cousin. "I'm so sorry. I didn't mean to make a commotion in your café."

Sonya and Heath opened Coffee & Claws together three years ago. The only business in Folk Haven co-owned by mythics from two different groups. A siren and a bear shifter. They make it work. Sonya handles the money and the staffing and is more of the business side of the café while Heath sticks to the food and makes sure they have the best coffee beans in the state, if not the whole East Coast.

Coffee & Claws is a staple of the town, and I had to go and cause drama in the middle of the dining area while working the job Sonya had definitely not needed to give me.

"If I upset anyone, I'll happily apologize." Even if it's that rude-as-hell Seamus. I can take the hit to my pride to make sure I don't screw over my cousin.

But Sonya waves me off. "No. No way. Heath told me the

whole story. You were in the right, no question." She steps in and wraps me in a sudden soft hug that somehow fills my eyes and throat with tears. "That must have been scary, seeing a guy choke like that. I'm proud of you. Probably saved his life."

This supportive affection is not something I'm used to. Not that I come from an unloving family or anything. Only my mother's way of telling me she loved me involved ending a work shift with constructive criticism. There were plenty of stressful days I would have preferred a firm hug and reassurance that I had done my best.

"I shouldn't have yelled at him." My claim comes muffled by the soft cotton of Sonya's indigo-scented T-shirt, which I've buried my face in.

"He should've thanked you. Or at least kept his mouth shut." She steps away, her hands bracing on my shoulders. "He had no right to yell at you."

Staring into my cousin's brown eyes—the color a few shades darker than Seamus's—I'm immensely glad that despite the difference in our appearances, Sonya and I are still blood family. Our mothers are sister sirens, but while my dad is as blond and pale as white corn, Sonya's father gifted her with the dark hair and tanned skin of his Honduran roots.

Mirroring our dissimilar appearances, we've also lived different lives. I grew up suppressing my mythical heritage at the urging of my parents while Sonya's was fostered with joy as she grew up in Folk Haven. Finally, after years of her urging, I decided to run to the family that accepted me for what I was as opposed to trying to mold me into something the human populace would find acceptable.

Hopefully, one day, I can embrace my siren half as easily as my cousin does.

"He was scared." I focus on the conversation at hand, not sure why I'm defending Seamus when I've decided to privately refer to him as Mr. Assface from this day forward.

Sonya's mouth twists. "How much did your parents teach you about selkie lore?"

That answer is easy. "Zero."

The most my mother ever did was list off the mythical creatures that existed in our world, but that was more of a warning. I wouldn't be surprised to find she left off plenty she didn't think was worth mentioning.

"Stay secret, stay safe," was her motto.

Her caution wasn't unfounded in relation to humans, but I never understood why we couldn't interact with others of our kind. Why we couldn't be honest for at least a small portion of our lives.

"Well, there's this one important part. Here, I'd better sing it." Sonya straightens up, and I hold my breath, readying myself for the beautiful notes.

She doesn't disappoint.

The Finned One worked
With power and craft
Formed the fragile
Selkie from glass

Should they break
The world would weep
But safety lies
In a lover's keep

When saved from harm
A mate is known
Their fate is found

The future shown

Sonya blinks her eyes open, having closed them while singing. "The original version was in Old English. That's a translation with some artistic flair our grandmother wrote."

A flicker of nostalgia alights in my chest at the hazy memory of a woman with hair whiter than mine, singing lullabies to me when I was a young girl. She passed away before I could get to know her, and since the woman was a siren, Mom doesn't talk about her much.

Sonya must have plenty of stories and songs in her head, celebrating Grandma Onassis. When I left my old life, I decided to follow the mythic tradition of taking a mother's last name even if my mother doesn't follow the same.

Good-bye, Neri Parker. Hello, Neri Onassis.

Unfortunately, this new magical me is dealing with new magical problems.

"So, Seamus thought me saving him somehow means I'm his mate?" Which caused him to react like I was a swamp monster come to steal his dick and balls.

Great. Don't I feel like the belle of the ball?

Sonya grimaces. "Guess the guy prefers single life."

The weird thing is, I could have sworn there was attraction on his part too. That the selkie was performing his own kind of awkward flirting. Guess I misread everything.

Apparently, the idea of mating me has him wishing I'd left him to suffocate.

"Fuck him," I mutter, not regretting my actions, but wishing I could take back those few flowery moments I mooned over him before that cookie tried to off him.

"Don't worry. There are plenty of good men in town. And women. And theys." Sonya gives me a suggestive nudge that I bat away. "Besides, you'd be better off with a human. No need to deal with the whole monster stigma."

That's at least some lore I know. When two mythics of different species mate, there's no predicting what their offspring will be, so they're just called monsters. Humans, on the other hand, tend to produce the type of mythic they mate with. Like our magic overwhelms their normalcy. That's what happened with my parents anyway. Mother is a siren, dad is a human, and I take after my mother.

And she worked to make my romantic life mimic hers. The thought has me grinding my teeth, residual anger lingering from the last time we spoke.

"All of this is moot." I reclaim my wine and wander toward the door leading to the screened-in porch, my cousin following. "I'm not looking for a relationship. I need more me time before I can consider anyone else." With a sigh, I pull out my ponytail and ruffle my short blonde locks, knowing there's a strange bump in them from being up all day.

"That's my girl." Sonya loops her arm around my shoulders and pulls me toward the steps that connect with a stone path through her backyard. "Let's go for a swim. Jumping in that water after a hard day's work is the best feeling in the world." She bobs her head back and forth. "Second best. Flying is better. But being in the water is pretty close."

"Sure." My relief brings a grin to my face. I really thought she was going to be mad at me. With a quick gulp, I polish off my glass of wine. "I just need to grab my suit."

Sonya chuckles. "Oh, my sweet, innocent cousin. This is the sirens' cove. You know what that means?"

I roll my eyes because after three weeks here, I've learned. "Yeah, yeah. Clothing optional. Sorry, I just can't get on board with skinny dipping when the sun is still out. I'll need to work up to that."

My cousin lets me go and saunters away. "Suit yourself. Bring a few beers when you come down. We'll swim over to Cassandra's dock for food. She's firing up the grill." I assume

Cassandra is another siren, and I make a note to remember her name. Sonya has introduced me to so many people, I'm struggling to keep names and faces connected.

"Okay." My cheeks tingle with the wide stretch of my smile that stays with me as I jog upstairs to change.

This is one of the reasons I asked Sonya if she had space for me when I fled the well-ordered life my parents had constructed. All my life, I'd exchanged letters and texts and phone calls with my cousin between our rare visits. As my mom pulled me more and more into the human world under the guise of safety, Sonya had detailed the tempting, freedom-filled life in Folk Haven.

My dreams filled with the sparkling water she'd sent me pictures of. Lonely nights in my apartment, I spent wishing I could be sitting on the end of a dock with her and all the other sirens in the cove where she lived.

My heart broke every day from wanting it so much.

And now, I'm here.

But there's something that keeps me apart. A thin yet impenetrable curtain, separating me from the life I've coveted. Some of my joy fades as I experience the push of the blockage now. This barrier between me and the freedom Folk Haven promises, which I haven't found a way to pierce.

And I'm afraid if I don't figure out how, one day, I'll have to leave.

4

———

SEAMUS

"What are you making?" As I stroll into my parents' kitchen, I rub my hands in anticipation, eyeing the baking ingredients my mother has spread over the counter.

Even a day after the disaster at Coffee & Claws, my body still rolls with high tension, as if the adrenaline never dissipated. Sorcha MacNamara's baking is more soothing than aloe on a sunburn, and I'm ready for the antidote to my anxiety.

"*I'm* not making anything."

Well, that sounds ominous.

Mama gives me a look she's used my entire life—the one letting me know I've fucked up. One would hope that the amount of knee-jerk guilt it inspires would be less now that I'm a thirty-two-year-old man.

But no.

"Is something wrong?" Even as I ask, I eye all available exits, wondering if I should run.

"Is something wrong?" She scoffs, throwing my words back at me as she aggressively ties back the curly hair she passed down to her four children. "How about one of my sons thinking it's just fine to holler at an innocent waitress for no good reason? You think that might be what has me fighting mad?"

My whole body wants to cringe, but somehow, I keep the reaction at bay, stiffening my spine. "That's oversimplifying things."

Who knew brown eyes could burn so hot? The MacNamara matriarch is not a woman to cross.

"Oh, I'm gonna make things real simple for you. You are going to go to her house and apologize."

"What?" My fists land on my hips. I'm ready to fight back even though I've never won an argument against my mother. "No. Definitely not."

Wrong thing to say.

An angry red flush fills my mother's cheeks, and she spears me with all of her Southern woman righteousness.

"That sweet girl is new to town. Just trying to find her way. And in the middle of a hard day of work, she takes the time to *save your life.*" The finger she pokes into my chest hurts like a baseball bat to the ribs. "That's right. Mrs. Morris was there, getting herself a coffee, and she saw the whole thing. Told me just how disrespectful and ungrateful my son was." Some of the heat fades from her voice, leaving an almost-weary air behind. "I have never been so ashamed."

Why not take a knife out of the drawer and gut a man with it?

Everything she's laying on me is right, but I can't help the defensive comment that jumps out of my throat. "I'm not going to mate her just because she gave me the Heimlich."

For a moment, my mama takes on the appearance of a freshly caught fish, mouth popping open in disbelief. Then, her nostrils flare on a deep breath, and I know I should've run when I had the chance.

"Did she ask you to be her mate?" She bites out the words.

"Well ... no. But if I go over there—"

"You mean, if you act like the decent person I hope I raised you to be, this woman is just gonna throw herself at you?" Mama huffs, shaking her head as disappointment cascades off her in waves. "I swear to The Finned One, you are more hung up on this mating lore than anyone else. You need to get over it."

"I need to get over it?" Now, I'm the one spluttering, as if freshly caught. "You're the one always talking about mates! Telling the story of how Dad saved you in that car accident and how you knew instantly that he was your fated mate."

The term *mate* isn't what I have a problem with. I'm not opposed to the idea of having a long-term, committed partner. Someone to share a home with, and trade secret loving looks with, and get tangled up in a bed with every night. An image of Neri floats through my mind, of the siren wearing only sheets and holding her hand out to me.

I shake my head to clear the thought.

No, mates aren't the problem. It's the *fated* part that sets my pulse hammering. The idea that the gods have some master plan, and when they give us a subtle hint of what they want, we're then expected to follow without question.

No matter the cost.

I've seen what that can do to a selkie.

My mother rolls her eyes. "He was working as a paramedic. He *had* to save me. And, yes, he was the handsomest man I'd ever seen. And, yes, I fell in love with him and married him. It's a good story, and it matches with our lore, but I didn't propose to him while he had me strapped to a gurney." She leans against the granite counter, a bag of sugar crinkling when her side presses against the ingredient.

"You asked him out on a date," I grumble.

From Mama's half-smile and distracted look, I know she's

reliving the memory. "He was so surprised. I can still remember that nervous chuckle he gave."

"This is what I'm saying." Waving a hand at her love-struck look, I take a defensive step back. "I'm not going to go over to Neri's house to have her moon over me."

Suddenly, the image comes to my mind. The beautiful siren staring up at me with a similar devoted look, as if I were the most precious person in the world to her. Oddly, my panic from earlier isn't the first emotional reaction. Instead, I experience something like excitement.

Which is ridiculous.

My mother's attention snaps back to me, a scowl returning to her normally smiling mouth. "If anyone should be mooning, it should be you over her. From what I hear, Neri is smart, hard-working, and ... oh, what was that other thing I heard?" She taps her chin, as if shuffling through her thoughts before snapping her fingers. "That's right! A *hero*."

Mama straightens, her eyes softening as she reaches a hand to gently cup my face. "I think all of my children are precious gifts from the gods and deserve everything they want in the world." The tenderness hardens in her eyes. "But right now, I'm reevaluating because a man who acts like you did does not deserve a woman like her."

My gut tightens in a knot I don't want to admit has been tied ever since the moment I first shouted at Neri.

"Mama—"

"Now," she cuts me off, "you are going to apologize. And not because you're looking for your mate. You will apologize because you were rude to someone who had done you a great kindness. In case you've forgotten in the last minute, I'll repeat, she *saved your life*. And"—Mama places a glass bowl in front of me—"before you deliver your heartfelt apology and thanks, you will whip up a batch of those dark chocolate brownies you're so good at. The Finned One knows you'll need to sweeten her up before she's ready to hear you speak again."

My mother goes to leave but pauses in the doorway at the last moment. "Don't think I won't know if you don't go."

Then, she's gone, and I'm left, trying to shrug off her scolding and her warning.

She wants me to show up at Neri's house with baked goods?

Might as well go grab a diamond ring while I'm at it.

"I'll make the brownies," I mutter, reaching for the butter. "I'll make them for me."

And that is my intention as I melt the butter and mix it with the sugar. As I crack eggs into the bowl. As I preheat the oven and rip open the bag of chocolate chips.

Yet somehow, through each movement, a picture of Neri's face crowds my mind. Her smile. Her chuckle. The warmth of her reddened palm, abused by the espresso machine. The firm grip of her arms around my torso. The perfectly placed pressure to dislodge the chunk of cookie from my throat.

One second, I was fighting for my breath, panicking at the idea of drowning on dry land.

Then, she saved me.

"Damn it," I mutter as I stir the rich batter with a wide wooden spoon.

I know she's new to town. Coffee & Claws was a rare stop for me, except on the days I needed a premade sandwich. That was the café's only appeal for the past few years. Bread, deli meat, and condiments.

Then, Neri appeared, and the first day I spoke to her rises in my memory. The way her moonlight hair was twisted into braids, but the true glow came from the smile she directed up at me.

"What can I get you today?" she asked.

You, blared in my mind.

"Roast beef sandwich and Earl Grey tea." I managed to get the words out past my suddenly thick tongue.

"Good choice. I had that sandwich yesterday, and it was heavenly. What's the name?"

I had to swim out of the enticing pool of her eyes in order to answer. "Seamus."

"Seamus," she repeated, my name never sounding better. "I think I know how to spell that, but I don't want to make the classic barista blunder of butchering it. Oh gods, now, I'm alliterating. Can you tell it's my first day? I swear I'm an adult who's worked in food service before."

Her cheeks flushed a red so deep that I was sure I could feel the heat. Or maybe I was the one boiling.

"What I'm trying to say is"—she gave a self-deprecating chuckle —"could you spell your name for me?" Her silver eyes held mine. "I want to get it right. I want to remember you."

Did she mean for that last comment to carry so much weight?

Despite a real worry that I'd forgotten how letters worked, I somehow got the right ones out.

I'd never cared about Coffee & Claws until Neri changed the entire feel of the place with her kind smile and singsong voice and teasing comments.

And I yelled at her.

The wooden spoon clatters into the batter as my body cramps. I clutch at the sharp pain in my stomach as guilt stabs through me.

Gods, her face. I barely registered the hurt shadowing her slate gaze when I was floundering in my own panic, but now, my memory blares the image across my eyes.

I fucked up.

Mate myth or no, I need to see Neri again. Find a way to coax out that lovely smile and make sure I haven't ruined her attempt to be happy, building a life in Folk Haven.

Just so long as she knows, that life won't be with me.

5

———————

SEAMUS

"Oh, look. Someone left a bag of shit on my doorstep. But they forgot to set it on fire. Maybe I'll have to remedy that." Sonya stares at me with unconcealed disgust as she leans on her door-frame, arms crossed in a clear signal of *come any closer, and I'll nut-punch you.*

"I deserve that." I sigh.

Every time I replay my reaction, my guilt grows sharper. I don't think I was wrong in wanting to establish that Neri rescuing my life wouldn't result in me mating her, but I could have relayed that information in a tactful manner.

"You deserve worse. Why are you here?"

"I want to apologize. And I brought brownies." I hold up the Tupperware container. "Freshly baked."

Sonya's eyes narrow. "I should shove one of those down your throat. See how you like choking when my cousin isn't around to save your ungrateful ass."

This is not going well.

"I panicked and said things I shouldn't have. Is Neri here? I'd prefer to apologize in person."

"I bet you would." Sonya drags her gaze down my body. "You rethink wanting to take her as your mate?"

"What?" I stumble back a step. "No!"

Sonya sneers, "Good. You don't deserve her."

My mother's words sound strange, coming out of the siren's mouth, and shame washes through me in another wave, the ripples never seeming to truly dissipate.

"She did a kind thing for me, and I regret my reaction. Can you please"—I grit the word through clenched teeth—"tell me where she is? I swear I'll be on my best behavior."

Sonya levels me with a long, silent contemplation and then shrugs, waving a hand toward the back of her house. "She's on the dock. Since she's a grown woman, I'm not going to decide who she can and cannot see. But if you're a dick to her, I'll hear about it." The siren leans in closer, dark brown eyes turning black as they burn into mine. "And I'll make your life hell in this small town. You hear me, selkie?"

Keeping my jaw tight so I don't say any of the comebacks jumping around in my mind, I offer a stiff nod and then stride through the grass, knowing there's no way Sonya will actually invite me inside.

The backyard is a solid mass of trees, but through their trunks, I spy glimpses of the shimmering blue-green that is Lake Galen. Following a stone-paved path, I approach the shore. Sonya has one of the common docks with a covered space for her speedboat and a floating dock attached to the side. On that gently swaying platform, I spy Neri.

And I try not to choke—this time, on my tongue.

The barista lies belly down on the dock, head toward the water. She has on a string bikini, the thin aqua straps showing off every curve and dip of her body. Some parts are muscled while others are rounded, teasing at a softness fingers might sink into.

Neri has a body made to be drowned in.

Freezing a distance away, I mentally shove away the erratic spikes of lust and command my eyes not to linger on how the scant fabric of the swimsuit clings to the swells of her ass and sneaks between her thighs, barely covering—

Stop it! I yell at myself.

After some controlled breathing, I force my gaze away from the private place on her body and move forward again. To keep my attention occupied, I study her back, recognizing a set of straight, parallel lines that trace down her shoulder blades. Like scars carved into her from a surgeon's precise scalpel.

Neri, like all other sirens, was born with those marks. They hide their wings, carrying their second form with them underneath their skin. Unlike my kind. Our selkie halves are vulnerable, existing separate from us and therefore requiring protection. My ancestors had a greater struggle than we do today, having to protect their selkie skins before the time of fireproof safes. Their lives must have been constant stress and worry.

Sirens dealt with different issues. Religious zealots labeled the strange marks on their backs as witches' marks. More than one siren met a death meant for another species of mythic. But I bet the priests would have been happy even if they had discovered the mistake they'd made.

Though times are easier in some ways now, the advancement of technology requires a different type of caution. Which is why Lake Galen is such a haven. Less prying eyes than the rest of the world and multiple actual witches who specialize in protection spells.

As I make my way down the sloping bank to the dock, I wonder what Neri's wings look like. *Does she ever unfurl them here? Does she soar over Lake Galen at night?* Maybe during the night of the dark moon, when I also embrace the mythic part of myself. Next time, I'll have to breach the surface of the water and peer toward the sky to see if I might spot a siren among the starry expanse.

Thoughts of swimming and wings seep away as I approach the barista. Getting closer only gives me a better view of her sun-soaked skin and strong curves.

That ass. Gods, that ass.

The way her suit hugs the two cheeks, sloping over the curves, is more provocative than bare flesh.

Of course, if she were bare, I'd have the perfect view of her—

I shake my head, trying not to think about how her pussy is probably the same dusky-rose color as her lips.

Why hasn't she acknowledged me? My footsteps sound loud on the wooden boards of the walkway out to the dock.

When I get close enough to peer over Neri's shoulder, I realize the item in her hands has captured her attention.

A book.

Damn The Finned One's games. Is there anything sexier than a woman reading?

Before making myself known, I reach down and adjust my half-hard cock. Only when I'm certain Neri won't be able to tell the dirty route my thoughts have taken do I clear my throat.

Her head pops up, and she glances over her shoulder at me.

Aviator sunglasses cover her metallic eyes, but from the twist of her mouth, I can easily guess her emotions about my arrival.

"Hello." *When did my voice get so squeaky and high-pitched?* If I spoke this way in front of my class, the students would laugh me out of the room. I clear my throat a few times and make sure I have a deep tone before continuing. "I have brownies."

Too deep. Now, I sound like I'm trying too hard.

And there's absolutely no reason for me to be trying anything right now.

"I'm allergic," Neri says, turning her attention back to the pages in front of her.

The reaction throws me more off-balance than the floating dock. "To chocolate?"

"To assholes." She flips a page. "Better get out of here before I break out in hives."

My assumption that the siren would jump on my apology and happily mend fences, all to smooth the ground for a mating, was delusional. And I'm left standing here, reeling from her derision.

"You can leave the brownies," Neri informs me, focus remaining on her reading material.

"The brownies come with an apology." *Now, will she act like I expect?*

"I'd rather they come with a bottle of red wine."

Her snark has me oscillating between a smile and a frown.

The only conclusion I can draw is my initial warding off worked. I should be at ease around her now. No risk of a mate-hungry siren chasing after me.

So, why am I brainstorming ways to make her look at me? To smile at me?

Neri slaps her book shut and flips over, bracing her arms against the dock so she reclines back, gazing up at me through her opaque sunshades.

"Is this apology written in invisible ink somewhere? Because I'm not hearing anything."

"Yes, right." I move forward and set the brownies on the dock beside her towel, and then I stay crouched on her level because looming over her is a strange position for contrition. "Thank you for helping me. I'm scared to think of what would have happened if you hadn't."

Underwater, I can hold my breath for hours. Would that power have transferred to choking on food?

"I should've been grateful. Instead, I yelled at you, and that was a horrible thing to do. Even if I was panicking, I should've realized you were just being a decent person. I am really, truly sorry. Especially because I felt as though we were starting to be friends." *More than that, if my dick had any say in the matter.* "I hate that I ruined that."

Silence hovers between us as Neri stares forward, eyes unreadable behind their shield. But then her hand sneaks out, scooping up the container of dessert. She pops the lid off and grabs one of the brownies, biting into the soft brown pastry.

At the approving hum in her throat, my cock twitches.

"Who made these?" she asks after swallowing.

"Me. I did."

Neri nods, finishing her brownie in two more bites and then swiping the crumbs off her lips, which I was tempted to offer to help her with.

"Apology accepted. But to be clear, I don't want to be—and never wanted to be—your mate. In fact, consider me your anti-mate."

Something like a blow rams against my gut, and it's all I can do not to let out a grunt. Instead, I give a slow nod of understanding.

We're on the same page. Good.

Speaking of pages ...

"What are you reading? Must be good. You didn't even hear me walk up."

For the first time since I improperly swallowed that cookie, Neri smiles at me. Wide and so genuine that I'm tempted to sway forward to get a closer look.

"Yeah. I just found this new historical author. I've been devouring her books."

Historical fiction? I've read some of the genre, but I haven't truly dived in. I tend to pick up thrillers and mysteries, but I'll try most anything. "Can I see?"

The second I get a look at the cover, I realize I misunderstood the genre. With a shirtless man sprawled on an ornate lounge, half-covered by a woman in a yellow gown, this is clearly a different sort of historical.

"Ah. Romance." I huff a laugh. "Guy lost his shirt, huh?" I grin at Neri, only realizing she's moved to stand. Rising alongside her, I hand the book back.

She accepts it, her hand retracting slowly. "You don't want to read the back cover?"

"I'm good. Not really interested. Too fluffy for me."

"Fluffy," she repeats the word, and I think to explain further, mind on the gritty crime novel sitting on my bedside table back at home.

"It's just that I'd rather have more meat to my books. An engaging story that hooks me. Something that digs deeper."

Neri's face reveals nothing, and I want to take those sunglasses off, so I can at least look into her eyes.

"Let me get this straight." She rocks back and forth, heel to toe. "You came here to apologize. And the second I let you off the hook, you think it's a good idea to insult my book. Does that sound about right?"

"What?" I yelp the word out. "No! I just meant that romance novels aren't my thing. I prefer something more serious."

The siren nods in a jerky way that makes me think I'm digging myself deeper into a hole of my own making. "I get you. My favorite genre is a bunch of fluffy nonsense, right? No wonder really since romance authors are mainly women."

"I'm sure some men write romance too," I automatically point out and then immediately cringe. *That's the part of her statement my brain chose to fixate on?*

When Neri lets out a sharp exhale of disbelief, I try to figure out how I screwed myself over so thoroughly. But I don't have much time to draw a conclusion because, suddenly, I'm tumbling off the dock.

I hit the water with an inelegant smack, my body sinking below the surface. The dunk, though surprising, is also oddly refreshing.

She pushed me, I realize belatedly as I allow my limbs to fully relax into the cool embrace. *I deserved it.*

That shame, paired with the wildly comfortable feeling of being fully immersed, has me pausing instead of trying to return to the surface. Everything is softer here, in the waters of Lake Galen. How long has it been since I last swam? On the dark moon, I take on my selkie form and swim all night. That's a certain type of release.

But swimming in my human form? It's been a while.

In the evenings, I'm usually grading papers or mapping out lesson plans. During the days, I'm teaching or attending department meetings or advising my students. Sometimes, I'll go over to my parents' house, but I always turn down my siblings' coaxing to join them for an evening dip.

It's been too long since I just ... floated.

My peaceful rest splits apart at the crash of bubbles beside me. When the turbulent water clears, I spy the gorgeous form of Neri next to me.

The siren reaches out, grabbing my face between her firm hands. In the cool water, her touch alights through my body, begging me to draw her closer.

Steely-gray eyes, no longer blocked by those massive sunglasses, stare into mine, and I can't help the way my mouth curves, enjoying finally being able to meet her gaze.

6

NERI

Mr. Assface is fine.

When Seamus didn't immediately resurface, I thought maybe I'd done him some actual harm. That I'd found the one selkie who couldn't swim and signed him up for an untimely death when I pushed him into the water. Or maybe the guy had hit his head on the way down.

But no. Here he is, grinning at me like he's having the time of his life, scaring the shit out of me.

Ridiculous.

And damn him for looking so handsome with that cheerful expression on his face.

There's a brush against my waist, and I glance down, expecting to find a fish. Instead, I spy Seamus's hand through the murky water, fingers grazing up my bare side. My nipples tighten in response, rudely not consulting me on the matter. Good thing I didn't give in to Sonya's encouragement to try skinny dipping or else he'd see exactly what that stroke does to me. His other hand finds my lower back, fingers spreading over the expanse of nude skin.

Did he just trace my bikini string?

In the same way I don't want to admit a smile transforms Seamus's face into something distracting, I also don't want to admit that his touch brings on a flare of lust in my body. A craving in my chest coaxes me to draw closer. To let my hands tangle in his wet curls or drag down his neck.

What would it be like to press myself against him? I imagine his solid form at my front while the gentle pressure of the water cradles us from every other angle. I've never thought about how the lake touches between my legs. How I have pressure on my center simply from immersing myself.

What would happen if this selkie replaced the water with the firm caress of his palm?

Luckily, I don't have to discover if I'd give in to the urge because, unlike a selkie, sirens can't stay underwater for extended periods of time. My lungs protest at the pause in their work, and breathing becomes much more important than exploring the unwanted feelings Seamus inspires in me.

With a final warning glare, I push away from him, kicking to the surface and gasping in a deep breath when my head pops above the water. Seamus follows a moment later, shaking water out of his eyes before seeking mine out.

The man's face sobers, no doubt under the weight of my glare.

"I'm sorry." His tone sounds serious, but I know better than to trust him.

"You said that before. Funny how it's hollower now." I swim to the dock and heave myself out of the water, praying to The Winged One my swimsuit bottoms stay in place during the exit.

"Neri—"

"Don't insult my book," I cut him off, pointing a warning finger at his floating head. "And if you don't want me to save you, then stop acting like the damsel in distress." With aggressive movements, I snatch my towel and dry my hands off enough to keep my novel free of water damage when I grab it.

Briefly, I consider abandoning the brownies. But the chocolate flavor lingers on my tongue, and I am weak enough to want another taste. I add the Tupperware container to my armful, slide on my sunglasses, and slip my feet into flip-flops.

All the while, Seamus remains floating in the water. Maybe he's worried I'll nut-punch him if he gets out.

He insulted my book, so nothing is off the table.

"I swear I wasn't trying to be a condescending ass," he says before I can escape.

That has me sneering down at him. "So, it just comes naturally to you? Fantastic." I toss my towel over my shoulder and give him my stone face, thankful for the added protection of my sunglasses. "Just because we live in the same town doesn't mean we need to interact. You stick to your selkie cove or whatever you call it, and I'll do all my fluffy, feminine reading here, where you don't have to suffer through the knowledge that I'm turning my brain to mush by reading stories that emphasize female pleasure and healthy romantic relationships. When you get your tea, I will treat you like any other customer. Sound good? Great." I answer my own question without waiting for his response and stride off the dock, uninterested in watching him climb out of the lake.

No need for me to see the way his clothes cling to him or the flex of his muscles as he rises from the water. Definitely don't need to track how the droplets trail down the exposed skin on his neck and arms.

My lower belly gives a pleasurable and unwelcome clench at the thought.

7

———

NERI

"YOU LOOK LIKE YOU NEED A SHOT." Zelda, my cousin's best friend, grins at me as she pulls a bottle of vodka out of the freezer.

Finding the intimidatingly beautiful Black woman in Sonya's kitchen is a common occurrence. Lots of sirens move freely in and out of each other's houses. I've yet to decide how I feel about that level of closeness. Especially when I forgot to remove my not-waterproof mascara before diving into a lake to save a selkie from drowning.

Save a selkie from drowning? Gods, I might as well be a human.

If I tell Sonya I jumped in after him, she'll pass out from laughter.

I can only imagine what raccoon state my eyes are in for Zelda to immediately offer alcohol. Interacting with Seamus MacNamara is a viable reason to drive me to drink.

"Maybe later." I wave my thanks and jog up the stairs.

After cleaning my face and changing into dry clothes, I

navigate through my many piles of unpacked belongings, trying to remember where I put certain items when I initially cleared out my apartment for the move.

I should've written more than the word *Books* on the box because I have a good thirty boxes labeled *Books* and no idea which one contains the sequel to the novel I'm about to finish. With a groan, I collapse back on the bed, bouncing as I land.

You know what would help? Buying new books. Then, I'd know exactly where they were.

"No. No more books," I tell my brain out loud to stop its tempting whispering. "Right now," I amend.

"You know you can unpack these, right? I'll even help." Sonya appears, staring down at me from over one of the box towers.

Her comment isn't pointed or judgmental, but I still feel a rise of self-consciousness, followed by guilt that I'm being ungrateful. When I wanted somewhere to run, Sonya opened up her house to me. No end date included. If anything, my cousin has acted like this could be a long-term arrangement for me.

But I don't even know if Folk Haven is long- or short-term. Until I figure that out, I'm not committing to the Herculean task of unpacking and arranging all my books.

"I'll think about it. But it's a lot, and they're fine where they are for now."

She smirks, seeing through my tissue-paper excuse.

"Okay. Live in your cardboard-box fortress then." With quick steps, she navigates the maze and collapses on the bed beside me. "How'd things go with Mr. Ungrateful?"

I shrug. "The brownies are good."

"We'll give him that then. He didn't yell at you again, did he? I'll make a purse out of his ball sack if he did."

"Oh gods!" I clap my hand over my mouth, failing to stifle

the chortling. "Please don't. I won't be able to hang out with you anymore if you're swinging around a testicle purse."

Sonya pokes my side, and I meet her eyes. She's smiling, but concern still hangs heavy.

"He apologized," I admit. "And it was a decent apology. But he still gets on my nerves."

And under my skin, which then makes my nerves feel things they shouldn't.

"Yeah. Seamus missed out on the charming gene. He's always been the stodgiest of his family."

Stodgy? That doesn't describe the man who traced my skin under the water, as if he had all the time in the universe.

"Moira, his sister, is intense but cool. His brothers are nicer. Have you met Calder? He comes into the shop more now that he's mated to Delta."

"Oh, I know her."

Delta Novac spends at least two days a week at the café, claiming a table and working on her dissertation and the online classes she teaches. The woman is a nerdy kind of gorgeous with her black hair usually tied in a messy bun and a set of glasses always sliding to the tip of her pale nose. A few times, a stocky white man has bought an Almond Joy latte from me and then gone over to set it on her table. The first instance, I thought he might be trying to come on to a hardworking woman. But then the professor grabbed the man by the shirt and pulled him in for a swift kiss that left him blushing.

The guy must be Calder. He certainly seems more jovial than his brother. Always leaves a good tip. Belatedly, I realize the brothers share the same curly brown hair that neither bothers to tame.

"Calder's nice," I admit. "I guess I can't write off the entire selkie population."

Sonya and I share a grin before hers goes softer. "There are some bad eggs in Folk Haven. Just like anywhere else. But I hope you won't let them drive you out." She snags my hand and draws it up to her mouth, kissing the back of it with a dramatic smack. "Things are better with you here."

I want to believe her. I really do.

But it's hard when there's so much unbalance in our relationship. All I know is that this arrangement has to be temporary. I want to find my footing in Folk Haven, but it's never going to happen when I'm relying on Sonya for everything.

"Thank you. Things feel better now that I'm here too." And it's the truth.

Despite the conflicting emotions battling within me now, the uncertainty is nothing compared to the discomfort, even pain, of living the life I had before. The one my parents had mapped out for me.

"You come down when you're ready. I'm going to hide the rest of the liquor from Zelda and then turn on the grill. Thought we'd have burgers for dinner."

"Sounds good. I'll be down soon." I wave her out and then go back to staring at the ceiling.

There's no use in moping over a selkie who showed his true colors, so I might as well forget him and ...

My phone buzzes. I try not to scowl when I see who the text is from. But then I unlock my screen and have to grit my teeth to keep from growling.

Mom: Call me. We need to talk about you coming home. Ronald will take you back.

Of course, she can't look past the end of my relationship to the real problem. That I don't want any part of the life she built around me, caging me in.

I set down my phone without responding. At some point, I'll answer with a quick *no*, but even that seems like giving her too much at the moment. Instead, I push aside a few boxes until I find the one labeled *Pants*. Popping the top flaps open, I reach in and pull out a pair of designer jeans. The kind that costs hundreds of dollars and fits like a perfectly tailored glove. The kind that has one of the few brand labels my mother approved of and allowed me to wear on the rare days I could dress casually in my rigidly structured past life.

Crawling over to a small desk in the corner, I snag a pair of scissors. The slide of the blades through denim calms my angry, racing pulse.

After finishing my craft project, I return to my ceiling contemplation, wearing a new set of cutoffs.

What am I going to do with the rest of my life?

Thoughts of Delta and her profession have my brain considering an idea.

School.

My business degree was a perfectly good choice for that other life I was expected to live, but now, with every other option in the world open to me, I'm wondering if I should try something different. I always enjoyed my time in the classroom.

A sense of purpose inflates my chest, and I roll over, reaching for the tablet I left on my bedside table. I search for Ramla University, the school located not too far south of town. A small liberal arts institute that, like Folk Haven, mainly serves mythics. I remember begging my parents to go to the place as I approached high school graduation. But surrounding myself with mythical beings didn't suit their idea of fitting in with the human world.

I didn't even bother filing my application.

Now, as I find the university's website and scroll through the different majors offered, I experience that spark of anticipation I had back as a teenager. I'm taking back control. And I won't let anyone—especially not a stuck-up selkie who's too handsome for his own good—throw me off course.

8

NERI

"Hᴇʏ! You new? Don't think I've seen you in this class before."
A white guy with hair the color of aged book pages offers me a
charming grin as he settles into the chair to my right.

"Hi." I put on my customer-service smile to cover my
nerves. "I'm just auditing a few classes. Trying to see if I want to
take something here next semester."

After researching, I finally committed to coming to Ramla's
campus and attending some in-person lessons. This is the third
course of the day, and I'm still waiting for the click of rightness
to sound off in my brain. The *this is right* switch to flick, telling
me I've found the correct next step for my future.

Come on, brain. Click for me.

"Ah." He nods, giving me a look that I'm betting is supposed
to appear wise. "About to graduate?"

"From high school?" I squeak, staring at the guy who's probably a decade younger than me.

"You go to Folk Haven High, right? Local girl?"

"Oh my gods, no. I mean, my genetics thank you for the

compliment." Plus, the top-notch concealer I use daily. "But I've already gone through college once. I'm thinking about earning a second degree."

I fully expect my seat neighbor to ignore me now that I've exposed myself as the—gasp—older woman that I am. Instead, the young man smiles wider and props his chin on his fist, gazing at me in a way that has me thinking he would not mind in the least being my boy toy.

"Sorry for the mistake. My bad. I'm Jensen, by the way."

He holds out his hand, and I shake it.

"Neri."

"Neri. That's a beautiful name. How do you like it here? I'm happy to answer any questions. Maybe give you a tour."

Oh yeah. This guy is definitely into me. Too bad I have no interest in sleeping with someone who I doubt can drink legally and who almost certainly lives in a dorm room that smells like Cool Ranch Doritos and weed.

Ten years ago, I would have gotten my flirt on hard. But now, I'm more interested in the lesson than romance.

"I'm getting the lay of the land." I use the vague answer to evade his invitation. "How do you like this class? Are you a public health major?"

Jensen nods. "Dr. MacNamara is cool. Tough but fair. And his lessons are always interesting."

"Dr. MacNamara?" The name squeaks out of me.

When I scanned through the course offerings, I just looked at the names of the classes and the days and times they were offered. I didn't think to look at who was teaching them.

Please, let it be someone else from the MacNamara clan.

Jensen keeps chatting, something about his public health major, but I struggle to pay attention as I eye the doors.

Should I leave?

But what if it's not him?

The click of a knob turning draws my attention to the front of the room. An entrance I didn't notice opens and reveals him.

Mr. Assface.

Or more accurately, Professor Assface.

Damn The Winged One's tricks.

Seamus strolls into the room, an air of authority clinging to him. The selkie immediately heads to the podium and fiddles with a computer there to start up the projector. All the while, his confident voice rings through the room, doling out instructions that his students hurry to follow, all of them pulling books and papers out of their bags.

I, meanwhile, sink lower in my seat and tug down the brim of my baseball hat.

Leaving is not an option. Even with his head tilted down, me standing would risk drawing his attention. And then where would I be? Caught running away from the pompous selkie.

No way in all the worlds will I let this man drive me out of a room.

Still, I keep my chin angled low, not looking forward to getting recognized either. Luckily, Water Quality Management of United States Lakes has a decent-sized enrollment for the small university. We're all scattered around this amphitheater, and I convince myself I'll be able to blend into the masses.

And for the first thirty minutes of class, I do. Seamus teaches his students without looking at them much. I find the method odd at first, but he doesn't seem to need to make eye contact to get them to take part. After a few instances of Seamus calling out names and people responding, I realize the selkie has at least a good portion of his students' names memorized. If the one he called on doesn't know the answer, then he simply moves on to someone else.

The practice interests me. Seamus doesn't shame anyone for not knowing the correct response, but by the random selection, it's clear that anyone could be asked to participate at any time. Keeps people on their toes. I even get to a point where I worry he's about to call my name.

Then, I remember he doesn't know I'm here, and I focus on trying to internalize the lesson. Not that I have any interest in taking Seamus MacNamara's classes, but I'm not about to give up on the idea of public health just because this selkie works for the department.

The problem is, I'm having a hard time reading the slides when Professor Assface keeps pacing in front of the screen. Not because his body blocks the words.

It's only that his pants fit him. Really well.

Seamus has on a set of khakis that skillfully map the curve of his ass.

Why can't he be the sloppy professor type with the tail end of his shirt hanging out?

But no. He tucked in his button-down perfectly, putting those taut globes on display.

And the shirt. That damn shirt. The stiff material hints at the strong shoulders underneath and hugs his solid torso. The buttons must be made of some kind of metal because they wink at me under the fluorescent light.

Teasing me.

Unbutton us, they whisper.

Damn those evil buttons. They're probably cursed by a bitchy witch who wanted to torment any woman who saw them.

I'm just guessing.

"Jensen. What are concerns surrounding Cyanobacteria blooms? And when do they most often occur?"

At the sound of my seat neighbor's name, all thoughts of clothing full of magic disappear, replaced with a spike of panic. In a rare moment, Seamus focuses on the theater-style seating, his stare seeking the guy to my right.

You're having a fun time with me, aren't you? I silently direct the sarcastic statement to The Winged One, sighing out my anxiety with my next breath.

I'm not surprised when Seamus's attention tilts to the side and catches on me.

As Jensen rattles on about some type of blue-green algae, I watch the professor's eyes go comically large. With close to an hour to deal with the shock of seeing this man where I never expected him, I find myself with the upper hand. Giving in to the urge to unsettle him as much as he's done me, I offer a subtle salute and smirk, sending him a silent message with the gesture.

Yeah, I'm here. Deal with it.

Hush descends over the class, and a full count of five goes by before Jensen's nervous voice pipes back up. "Did I miss something?"

Seamus shakes his head, ripping his eyes away from me and bouncing them all around the room. "No. Good. That was good. Yes, um ... where were we?" He clears his throat once and then twice, staring at his slides for a touch too long before starting back up with the lecture.

As the hour finishes, I'd bet all my books that Professor Assface has glanced at me at least once a minute. I press a fist to my mouth to hide my gleefully triumphant smile.

"That's good for today." Seamus shuts down the projector screen. "Remember, final papers are due in two weeks. Come by during my office hours if you'd like feedback on your drafts. Next week will be a review."

Students pack up, and I realize that my buffer is leaving.

"So, about that tour?" Jensen stands and stares down at me, hopeful smile on his wide face.

"Thanks for the offer, but I'm going to stick around." An evil chuckle plays through my head. "Chat with the professor."

The guy's smile dims, but he offers a friendly wave and

heads out. I wasn't feeding Jensen an excuse. Leaving without a word might as well be running away.

Besides, the selkie has come into my space and set me off-balance multiple times.

Time for revenge.

9

_____

SEAMUS

She's here.

She's walking toward me.

What do I do with my hands?

I've never had to consider their placement before, but after letting the pads of my fingers stroke over her bare skin, that's the only place they want to be. And they definitely cannot be there. I'm at a loss.

With her steps away, I panic and hook my thumbs in my belt loops.

Like I'm a cowboy.

Gods, I'm a mess.

"So, you're a professor? I was thinking accountant, but this fits better." Neri runs her silver gaze down my body, no doubt making note of my odd hand placement.

"You think I'm a good professor?" I tend to score well on my student evaluations, but for some reason, I want to hear praise from the siren's lips. I consider showing her the Rate My Professor page, where multiple students have assigned me a chili pepper icon that identifies me as hot as well as good at instruction.

Wait ... what? No. Don't do that.

Neri tilts up one shoulder, and I realize the last of my students has stepped out the door. Leaving the two of us alone.

"I said, this fits better. You know, that whole academic-arrogance thing." She affects a nasally voice, mockery in every syllable. "I don't have time for genre fiction. Not when there are so many classics written by boring white men to read."

I cringe. Seems her acceptance of my original apology has not extended to my post-fuckup.

"I'm sorry. I shouldn't have insulted your book." Silently, I curse my past self for all my uneducated knee-jerk blunders. I clear my throat and scramble for a way to redeem myself. "Are you interested in the public health program here? We'd be happy to have you. The faculty is top-notch. I can introduce you around." Arrange for her to talk to someone who she doesn't already loathe.

I hate the idea that I'd drive someone away from attending school. Knowledge is glorious, and everyone should take part in gaining more.

"Haven't decided yet. I'm auditing a few different classes. My first degree is in business, but I'm not sure if I want to stick with a program that pairs well with that or veer off into new territory." Neri says all this to a sheet of paper in her hands, voice thoughtful, as if she's talking more to herself than to me. "Maybe English."

"So, you can read a bunch of classics by boring white guys?" I keep my voice deadpan, and her responding smirk does strange things to my gut.

"Maybe."

Finally, I unhook my thumbs and hold out open hands in hopes that the gesture conveys my sincerity. "Don't toss out public health just because of me. There are a lot of directions to take in the major. And if you do end up in one of my classes, I promise we could maintain a respectful teacher-student relationship."

Neri stares at me, her iron irises sending an unexpected warmth trickling down my spine.

"I don't think that will work," she says.

"Why not?"

After a long, heavy pause, Neri opens her mouth.

The heat shoots straight back up my spine and into my brain, filling my mind with bright rays of pleasure. When I blink, I feel like I'm waking in the middle of an amazing dream that I can't remember with a teasing in the back of my skull that I was about to do or say something very important.

No, that's not it.

Neri said something very important. Something beautiful.

What was it?

"What did you just say?" I step toward her, drawn to her, and wobble on unsteady feet.

She matches my approach by skipping back two paces of her own. "I didn't *say* anything."

The taunting emphasis on that one word clarifies things.

"You sang." The siren must have crooned her last words. That's the only explanation for my sudden amnesia. "You sang something to me. Just now."

Neri's mischievous smirk starts up an ache in my chest, but she doesn't bother admitting what we both know.

"Have a good day, Professor."

My body ripples with pleasure at my title in the lilt of her voice, but even that cannot distract me.

"Tell me what you sang," I demand as she jogs up the steps between the aisle of desks.

"You don't remember?" Neri taunts, throwing the comment over her shoulder.

Her refusal to answer has me growling a curse. She knows I

don't. That I can't. No one but another siren is able to remember what they sing in their haunting melodies.

"You're trying to enchant me," I snarl. The words come out before I think them through.

Neri freezes, only her swooping ponytail swinging as her body goes rigid, and yet again, a second too late, I realize I fucked up. The woman whirls on her heel, glaring down at me from her high vantage point, like a gorgeous, vengeful goddess.

"Wrong." The word whips between us. "A siren's song has never been an enchantment. It's simply beautiful. And private. We keep our secrets to ourselves. All the myths about my kind luring sailors to their deaths on the sharp rocks of our islands are lies. Covers for selfish immaturity."

When the steel of Neri's eyes touches me now, I wince at the cold slice of her disdain.

"Because men can't stand the idea that there's something they're not allowed to know."

Even when she's gone, the weight of her dismissal remains.

10

———

SEAMUS

I FIND myself in a similar position to the past but entirely unsure of my reception.

"Did I really need to come with you?" My sister glances up at me from the screen of her phone, but her eyes immediately drop back down. Her thumbs tap at a rapid pace, probably writing an email the same time she talks to me. Moira is a master multitasker.

"What do you mean, need to come with me? I invited you to lunch. That's what good brothers do."

I fiddle with the top button on my shirt, making sure my collar sits flat as I glance toward the dwindling line. The space between me and the Coffee & Claws front counter decreases.

Between me and the barista.

"Last time you took me to lunch was on my birthday. Six months ago." She slides her phone into an outside pocket on her purse and fixes me with an uncomfortably piercing gaze.

"It's not a big deal," I grumble. "If you didn't want to eat with me, you could have said no."

Moira smirks. "And miss out on you trying to act like you're a mature adult in front of the siren?" She leans to the side, obvious in her attempt to get a glimpse of Neri. "Mama told me about your tantrum."

"I didn't have a tantrum," I hiss, voice low, questioning why I thought bringing Moira would be a good idea. All I knew was that I wanted to see Neri again to set the record straight. And that backup might be helpful.

"Fine. Call it what you want." She straightens. "All I know is, this woman has you falling to pieces, and I'm looking forward to my front row seat."

I'm on the verge of coming up with a scathing retort when the customer ahead of us moves aside.

And there she is.

Instead of her normal baseball hat, Neri's crown is bare. Her white-gold hair twines into two braids curving along her skull, each one tied off just above her shoulders. I imagine her in front of a mirror this morning, clever fingers maneuvering the strands.

What would it be like to watch her morning routine?

"I think we're up. Or do you need a second to wipe away your drool?" Moira's drawl snaps me out of my thoughts, and I whip my hand up to my face to make sure no actual spit has creeped out.

"You're such a dick," I mutter.

"I'm a what?" At Neri's musical voice, I find her silvery gaze narrowed on me.

I have to swallow a time or two as I approach the counter.

"Nothing," I assure her. "You're nothing."

Her head jerks, and I want to bash my fist into my own face. Moira, the most unhelpful wingwoman the gods have ever fashioned, lets out a snort.

"That's not what I meant." In a desperate move, I grab my

sibling's arm and pull her forward. "I was talking to my sister. This is Moira. Moira, this is Neri."

"Please don't hold it against me that I'm related to him."

Moira holds out her hand, and Neri shakes it across the counter, a hesitant smile curving her lips.

A true smile. An easy, kind, playful one. The one I don't get from her anymore.

"You say that like I have a grudge against your brother, and I can't imagine why you'd think that." Neri grabs one of the twenty-ounce cups off the little tower. "It's him who can't stand me. Didn't you hear?" She grins wide, even as her eyes tell me to fuck off. "I'm constantly finding new and devious ways to trick him into a relationship."

I hang my head at that, my own voice echoing in my mind about how she tried to enchant me when I knew full well that was not how a siren's song worked. That wasn't even what I was mad about at the time.

I wanted to know what she'd sung to me.

No way will she tell me now.

"You know ..." Moira has her thoughtful tone on. The one she uses when planning things I don't particularly like. "You're my kind of bitchy. I'm a fan. Keep up the good work. And I'll have the avocado delight on sourdough, please. With a glass of sweet tea. And a bear claw, if Heath has some coming out of the oven soon."

Neri spares my sister a grin before typing on the register's tablet surface. When her attention turns to me, she still wears a smile, but the genuine note disappears. This is a customer service smile. An expression that lacks all authenticity. Behind it, she could be thinking about her grocery list, a doctor's appointment, or the dead body she needs to bury.

No doubt I'm the one going in the shallow grave.

"And for you?"

"Turkey and Swiss on whole wheat, please. And the tea." Even I can hear the strain in my voice.

Why did I have to go and mess up everything between us?

And why do I keep doing it?

When Neri returns my credit card, her attention immediately moves to the next person in line. Dismissing me.

I shuffle to the table Moira's settled at. My sister tries to pry me open with her eyes, and I stare everywhere but at her, doing my best not to let her crack me.

"I don't get you. I really don't." She reaches out to absent-mindedly straighten the small condiment selection living on the café table.

"I'm a complicated man," I offer.

She snorts. "Confusing does not equate to complicated. A man swimming in jean pants is confusing but not complicated."

"Who would swim in jeans?" The idea of all that wet denim weighing my limbs down is too horrifying to contemplate.

Moira shrugs. "Who would sabotage his chance with a funny, witty, beautiful woman just because he thought the gods approved of the match?"

I'm sputtering my way to a response when said woman's arrival at our table cuts me off.

"I have your sweet tea and avocado delight." Neri names the items as she sets my sister's order down. "And your Earl Grey and turkey sandwich."

The familiar steaming cup elicits a content glow in my chest, but then I get a look at my food and struggle to comprehend what's on my plate.

Neri leans in, holding her tray in front of her chest like the plastic acts as a shield between us. "Don't worry. I asked Heath to cut it into bite-sized pieces for you. Avoid choking hazards, you know? Gods forbid I have to save you again." With a final smirk, Neri flounces away.

Our table exists in a moment of silence. Moira breaks first with a loud bark of laughter. I glare at her, but that doesn't stop the hilarity.

"She's good. I want to hire her." Moira wipes a stray tear from the corner of her eye. "In fact ..." Not bothering to finish the statement, she slides out of her chair and strolls up to the counter.

I'm too far to hear any of the words, but I watch as my sister hands over a business card. Neri takes the offering with wide eyes.

"What was that about?" I ask when she returns to our table.

Moira takes a bite of her not-mutilated sandwich, chewing and swallowing before answering. "I told her to call me if she's looking for work somewhere other than here."

"She's thinking of taking classes at the university." My response is surprisingly defensive, as if Neri choosing the university were the same as her choosing me.

But why would that matter?

It's not like I want her to choose me.

Right?

"Maybe she'll want to earn her real estate license instead."

"Why would she want to do that?" I'm being a dick of a brother, but sometimes, that's what siblings do to each other.

Moira narrows her eyes but loses the expression a second later when Neri appears beside our table. Automatically, I straighten in my seat.

"One Coffee & Claws famous bear claw. Made by a real bear." The siren sets the treat down with a flourish. "Sorry. Heath makes us say that."

The bear shifter sticks his shaggy head out of the kitchen door and gives a thumbs-up.

"Thanks. Hold up a second." Moira's request stops Neri as the barista moves to leave. "I have a pressing question."

This can't be good. The devious glint in my sister's eyes tells me so.

"What's on your mind?" The siren tucks her hands into the pockets of jean shorts I wouldn't mind watching her swim in.

Moira flicks her gaze to me and then back to the siren, who seems to give off a subtle glow.

Am I the only one who notices?

"Would you let my brother take you out on a date?"

The world stills, frozen in the wake of Moira's question. Something crashes, and I realize it's the sound of my own heartbeat pounding in my ears.

I want to look at Neri, and at the same time, I want the floor beneath my chair to liquify, so I can sink out of this restaurant and swim to the safety of ignorance.

"I know about the"—Neri's hesitation is enough to draw my attention upward in time to catch her glance around the café —"traditions your family has. When it comes to choosing partners."

The odd wording confuses me for a breath until I realize she's attempting to be circumspect when discussing mating lore in public. Folk Haven's population is largely mythic but not entirely. And only some of the humans are aware of their magically inclined neighbors.

Neri continues, and I try not to show how closely I hang on to her words.

"My family doesn't have the same ... beliefs. Plus, there are the issues that arise when people from certain—different— families form an attachment."

Though her words are vague, both Moira and I know the issue she's referring to.

The monster stigma.

Not for the first time, I question why we'd apply such a negative title to children just because their parents were different mythics who fell in love and started a family. There are monsters who live on Lake Galen, and it's not like they're causing constant mayhem.

Not the friendliest bunch, but they have been judged their whole lives, so what should we expect? Add on the fact that their parents likely got backlash for making them, and I'm surprised monsters associate with other mythics at all.

"So, getting back to your question, I don't feel a higher force pushing me toward your brother, but I'm not opposed to dating someone just because other people think it's taboo."

A wild wave of hope rises in my chest. She swiftly dashes it against jagged rocks.

"However, if I were going to deal with that scorn, it wouldn't be for a man who ran away, screaming at the idea of being with me."

Neri reaches across the table to grip my cup. I half-expect her to dump the hot liquid on my lap, but instead, she gives it a ninety-degree turn.

"Enjoy your lunch," she says in an overly sweet tone that has my groin tightening.

Once she's back at the register, I tear my eyes away and study my drink, realizing Neri gave my name special treatment again—only this time, she took liberty with the spelling.

Shame Moose.

"I think we both know you deserve that." Moira emphasizes her point with a massive bite of her sandwich.

A blush of shame creeps under my skin as toxic regret pumps through my veins.

"Yeah," I mutter, "I know."

What have I done?

11

———

NERI

Sonya must have raided every office supply store in northern Georgia because there are more whiteboards in her house than the high school.

There are also more sirens than I realized who live on Lake Galen. At least, I assume the forty-plus people strewn throughout the first level are all sirens. My guess comes from the fact that half of the words are sung rather than spoken, and no one seems to be in a haze of confusion from forgetting what was just related.

The way Seamus looked when I trilled that verse off the top of my head on my way out of his class.

The move was immature. I know that.

But I felt an overwhelming urge to tease him. And I've held myself back from singing for so long, adhering to another of my parents' rules. When the silly rhyme popped into my head, I couldn't help myself.

So, I sang to him.

Your class is divine
Your ass is too fine
What could I study
With a butt so lovely
Captive in my eyeline

Innocent. Honest. Embarrassing.

And yet I understand his anger.

"Really shouldn't do that again," I mutter to myself as I maneuver through a crowd in the living room, trying to make my way to the kitchen, where I hear Sonya's voice.

My cousin stands in front of yet another whiteboard while a group sitting around the kitchen table shouts out different phrases that make absolutely no sense to me.

"The love cages! The witches still need to spell the metal," a woman with curling mahogany hair only a shade darker than her skin shouts out. I think her name is Nissandra.

My goal is to learn the names of at least everyone living in this cove by the end of next month.

The table cackles.

"Remember the 2015 Gauntlet?" someone shouts.

Sonya wears an evil grin as she writes *love cage spell* on the board under the title *To Do*.

"The werewolf and the dragon! That was priceless!"

"Did his finger ever grow back?"

"Don't think so."

The group shares a laugh at whatever strange inside joke they have. This whole event has me feeling lost. Like I missed an important memo.

"Neri!" My cousin's eyes alight on me, and she hands off her marker to Zelda, who takes over. Sonya makes her way to me, throwing an arm around my shoulders. "Things are coming together!" Her squeeze is all excitement and no clarity.

"What exactly is coming together?"

She guides me to the counter, where there are enough snacks to feed an army. "The Gauntlet, duh. Don't worry. Each planning meeting is held in a different house. We've got today, but next weekend, someone else's home will get invaded."

Still reeling and utterly confused, my attention snags on a piece of music drifting through the window. I peer outside to see Mona, a siren I met who works in the grocery store. She's reclined on one of the cushy lounge chairs on the porch and seems to be singing to herself as her hooded eyes remain shut.

Bars never stopped him
No hold on him
The selkie found Galen
They saved each other's lives

When I refocus on Sonya, she's cracking open a can of soda for herself.

"Feel free to join in. But since you just moved to town, you can definitely sit out of the planning this year if you'd rather be a spectator."

"I'm lost." I pull my own soda from the fridge and press the cool can against my neck, overheated in this crowded house. "A spectator for what?"

Finally, Sonya brings her focus fully to me. In my eyes, she must spy my true confusion.

"Wait. Are you telling me you've never heard of Galen's Gauntlet?" She says those two last words with an air of reverence. "Your mom never told you?"

With a grimace, I shrug. "If it's mythic-related, she doesn't talk about it."

"Gods. Well ..." Sonya's face eases into a grin. "Prepare yourself for a fun time. The Gauntlet is a competition we sirens, along with the witches, put on every two years. Part race, part obstacle course, part mindfuckery."

"Hell yeah!" Zelda crows from the other side of the room, lending support to Sonya's description with a fist pump.

"So, sirens race?" I ask.

"Oh no." She snorts and then sips her drink before answering. "We're the event organizers. The competitors are other mythics. We get a pretty diverse field. They have to pay to enter, people have to pay to watch, and the winner gets a fourth of the pot, plus other perks around town. And bragging rights." Sonya picks up a carrot stick, crunching into it as she talks. "I think half the entrants are just there for the title. It's a pride thing." She shrugs. "Whatever gets them coming back. We're a month out, and things are going to ramp up between now and the day of the Gauntlet."

"I never realized." Anticipation fills my chest at the thought.

A competition between a bunch of mythics? There was a time in my life I merely wished to have one person like me to talk to. Someone who knew the truth about my other half.

Now, I'm living in a place where there are enough people like me to hold full-blown events with only mystics in attendance.

Whatever wildness this Gauntlet is, I can't wait to be a member in the crowd.

Mona's song teases my mind, and I find myself stopping my cousin as she moves back toward the kitchen table. "Hold up."

Sonya turns her earthy gaze back to mine.

"What was that song Mona was singing? I haven't heard it before."

When her eyebrows shoot high, I know I'm in for a good story.

My favorite thing in the world.

Sonya pulls me farther away from the group, finding the quietest corner in the kitchen.

"How much do you know about Lake Galen?" she asks.

The sudden change in topic throws me, but I try to answer

as best I can. "Uh, I can navigate around it pretty well now. And I think I have a good idea of where each of the factions live. Is that what you're talking about?"

Sonya shakes her head. "I mean, how much do you know about the history?"

"Oh. Not much, I guess. I just know that a bunch of mythics settled here and in Folk Haven a while back and built it into a kind of refuge for us all."

Sonya gives me this wide-eyed stare that makes me feel like I'm missing something big. "Mythics didn't just settle here." She waves out the window, where I can spy a glitter of water through the tree branches. "They made the lake. They built Folk Haven."

"Really?" That seems like a lot of work. "I had no idea."

"That's what the song is about. The start of Lake Galen. But"—her face goes serious—"it's not a happy start. Your mom never told you about The Collector?"

"Is that a person?"

The siren's entire face scrunches in disgust, but from the way she glares out the window, I'm safe in guessing the sentiment isn't for me.

"A person. A sorcerer." She hisses the last word.

"Oh gods." I at least know what a sorcerer is.

Human born, they steal magic from mythics. A feat only achieved with twisted spells and lots of pain on the part of the mythical creature they're thieving from. One of the worst insults for a witch is to call them a sorcerer.

"Yeah. All sorcerers are horrible, but this guy was truly fucked up. He was from France originally but moved to America in the early 1900s. Bought up acres and acres of land. Built this huge estate." The can in Sonya's hand lets out a metallic protest as her fingers clench. "He also built cages. A menagerie. He caught mythics and kept them there. Kept them here really."

As Sonya talks, her words become less harsh and more melodic, eventually flowing entirely into a song.

And that's how I learn the story of The Collector.

And Galen.

The Collector did exactly as his name indicates. He collected mythics. With his massive zoo of our kind, he was powerful. Possibly the most powerful sorcerer who ever lived. But The Collector was also a man and could not deny his attraction and fascination with one of his captives.

A siren named Galen.

One day, he would treat her as a prized pet, offering her treats for good behavior. Other days, he would go into rages, punishing her and leeching power from her with his dirty spells. Then, other times, he would speak as though they were a couple. As if he loved her.

As if he even knew what that word meant.

Galen fought at first but soon realized she wouldn't be able to beat him through might. So, she began to play along. Pretend that she cared for him too.

What most often drove The Collector to anger was her singing. Like every other being in the world, he could never remember the lyrics of her song. Only that the words she'd sung were hauntingly beautiful.

Singing to The Collector kept Galen sane because in her songs, she would sing out all of her hatred for the vile man. The moment she closed her lips, he would forget, and so she was safe. The other thing that kept her sane was a selkie that The Collector kept. Their cages were close enough for conversation, and soon, the two fell in love.

The selkie did his best to offer her strength and comfort, but whenever The Collector took her from her cage, it was all the mythic could do not to bash his skull against the bars just to erase the thoughts of what the sorcerer did to her when she was out of his sight.

Eventually, Galen convinced the sorcerer that the only way he would be able to remember her songs was if they made love under a full moon with her wings extended. Until that moment, The Collector had kept an iron brace on her back to stop her from extending her wings.

Desperate to have everything that was hers, the sorcerer took her to an open space on his property, where the full moon shone down. He let her release her wings but then chained the edges to posts, so she wouldn't be able to fly away.

But Galen never had any intention of fleeing.

As the evil man took his pleasure from her body, she wrenched her wings against her bonds so hard that the bones snapped. The bound ends hung bloody from their shackles, and with the splintered limbs still attached to her back, Galen drove the bone spikes into the sorcerer's neck.

Under the full moon, the man drowned in his own blood, eyes locked on the siren who'd finally destroyed him.

Galen freed the rest of the mythics in the menagerie, and the creatures killed the few apprentices The Collector allowed on his property. When she finally unlocked her selkie lover's cage, he gathered her bloody, broken form into his arms, terrified the shattered wings meant she would die.

However, one of the prisoners was a healing witch and claimed she could save Galen.

But the price the spell demanded was steep. In the depths of The Collector's home, Galen's lover found his selkie skin. To revive the pieces of Galen's wings lost, he had to cut from his second skin and lay the pieces over her wounds, so the witch could mend the dying woman with a gift of true love.

The process was agonizing but worked.

Galen rose physically whole.

She and her selkie lover left The Collector's cursed estate, traveling far away to find a new home where their souls might heal together.

Some of the other freed captives followed suit, wanting as far from the place of their pain as they could get. However, a war waged in Europe, and homes that existed two decades before were not the same anymore. A group of mythics decided to claim The Collector's estate as their own.

But the land was steeped with his twisted magic. To cleanse the entire expansive property would require meticulous work by dozens of witches who mastered cleansing. They had none. However, the healing witch among their number knew of another way.

Water was the natural means of ridding a place of dirty magic.

It took years of work as well as legal maneuvering and land purchasing, using The Collector's hidden wealth, but finally, the survivors were able to construct a dam. With the massive structure in place, The Collector's tainted home flooded as well as a portion of the land surrounding it.

Lake Galen was born, named for the siren who'd broken their chains.

My cousin finishes the song with three verses that ring in my ears and into my heart, so I know I'll never forget them.

He tried to rule us
To collect us
He said he was the darkness
But the night is where we thrive

He's the beginning,
Not the ending
Galen he could not possess.
She's the reason we survive

So, swim deep,
And fly high
Dig your claws into the earth
Claim your freedom and your pride

Sonya's voice trails off in a haunting tune, and I realize the entire kitchen is silent. What was once a house full of noisy banter and excitement now is a collection of sirens with heads dipped in quiet respect.

"What happened to Galen?" I keep my voice soft as I ask.

Sonya shakes her head. "She and her selkie disappeared. North is the only direction they told anyone." A sad yet hopeful smile tugs at her lips. "I like to think they found their own lake. Or maybe a house on the coast and lived out the rest of their lives free. And at peace."

At peace. That is a nice thought, if unrealistic. The kind of trauma they endured doesn't disappear with the death of the villain.

"And so Galen's Gauntlet is …"

"Tribute!" Zelda shouts out, and the rest of the gathering roars in agreement.

My cousin leans in closer to be heard over the din. "Every other year, we pay homage to Galen's sacrifice." She tilts her head with a wry grin. "But sirens aren't ones to sit in stoic contemplation. So, we made the Gauntlet. And because Galen gave the most to free us, sirens act as game masters. The other mythics take part. Those who pay the entry fee."

"You said the winner gets money?"

"The money from entries and ticket sales gets divided four ways. The winner gets a fourth. The witches who provide warding and some of the obstacles for the competition get a fourth. We donate a quarter to the town for public program-ming. And then the sirens keep the last chunk for ourselves."

"Ourselves?" I imagine my cousin making it rain with some fat stacks of cash. "What does that mean?"

"There's a fund we have. A safety net. If a siren is ever in need of financial assistance, she can petition for a payment." A far-off look enters Sonya's eyes. "Money is power, and power is freedom. No siren will ever let another be chained again."

When my cousin meets my gaze then, understanding pierces my chest, and I fight the sudden pressure of tears.

She saw the chains of my past life. She offered me a way out. She gave me a key to my freedom.

And now, I can do anything I want with it.

12

————

SEAMUS

I'M WAITING for the librarian to retrieve my books on hold when an unexpected pressure encourages me to turn around. The urge is undeniable, my body shifting without me fully considering why.

She's here.

Across the collection of computer stations in the main area of the university library, I spy a familiar ponytail sticking out of the back of a baseball hat. The short white-gold mass swaying as the owner scans a bookshelf.

"Dr. MacNamara? Here are your titles." The librarian reappears at the desk with the stack of books I had shipped from another library.

"Thank you. Think I'll look them over before checking them out, if you don't mind."

She waves me to go ahead, and I scoop up the armful and then power-walk toward the siren, not sure what my plan is.

All I know is, I need to be near her.

To find out why she's here, of course. And then once my curiosity is satisfied, I'll leave her alone.

"Neri."

Her head jerks up at the sound of her name, and I shiver at the cold brush of her silver gaze. She rolls her metallic eyes and returns her attention to the shelves.

"Seamus." Her musical voice caressing my name has my groin tightening even if she did pronounce it as *Shame Moose*. "Here to judge my reading choices? Don't worry. This leisure section is sorely lacking in romance titles. I'm filling my fantasy obsession instead."

Neri holds a pile of hardbacks. With her arm blocking the spines, I can't read the titles, but if she's going for fantasy, then no doubt, I've read a few.

"I'm sorry." I wonder if there will be a day when I don't have to start off a conversation between us with an apology.

Neri's finger, tracing over the books on the shelf, pauses. But then she returns to her steady scanning, offering no response or witty sting.

So, I keep going. "Insulting an entire genre of books I hadn't taken the time to explore was wrong of me. And even if I'd read extensively within romance and still not enjoyed the books, I should never have insulted them but instead provided a well-informed critique that acknowledged the reasons why I personally was not a fan but had an understanding as to why there was a large portion of the population that was."

Yes, I did practice this speech in my bathroom mirror, hoping I would have an opportunity to deliver it. Having run out of the words I rehearsed, I go off script.

"I also think it is likely I would enjoy certain romance titles. If you take this novel, for example, while marketed as a science fiction adventure, there is a romance plotline." I clasp my academic texts in one arm, so I can pull the book off the shelf and hold it up for Neri to examine the detailed space scene on the cover.

Either the movement or the apology earns me the siren's brief attention. Her cool eyes flick between the book and my face and then back again.

"Does it have an HEA?"

"A what?" Curiosity spikes in my chest. A new acronym? For books? I must learn what it is.

"Happily Ever After. Or HFN, which is Happy For Now. Does the love story end on a positive note? With the lovers in a relationship that I can imagine extending past the last page of the book?"

"Isn't that giving away the ending?"

"I didn't ask you *how* the book ended. Just the note that a particular plotline ends on. Positive or no? If you're actually interested in the romance genre, you'll want to make note of this because it's one of the only two conventions required." She holds up a fist. "Central love story." One of her fingers extends. "HEA or HFN." Another finger.

The siren drops her hand, using it to shift her collection of reading material to prop on her opposite hip. I spy marks on her arms from where the heavy books have been digging into her skin.

"Can I hold those for you?"

"No." Neri waves her hand in front of my face and then points to her eyes. "Pay attention. I'm teaching you something."

"Yes. Sorry. Of course." I know better than to interrupt a lesson. Once again, I am Shame Moose.

"I read across genres, but if something is marketed or recommended to me under the guise of it being a romance, then it'd better have a happily ever after. If it doesn't, I'll be pissed. Just like every other romance reader would be. Just like I'm sure you'd be mad if someone handed you a book, called it a mystery, and the characters solved the crime in the first couple of chapters, and the rest of the time you were just reading about their lives or whatever. Genre conventions are simply categorization methods, and they're important for reader satisfaction. So, I'm asking you, is this book"—she reaches out and taps the cover of the book in my hand—"a romance?"

Thinking back on the ending, I word my answer carefully. "The love story is not the central plotline, but it does end on a positive note. So, it is a sci-fi novel with a minor romance plotline." My tone mirrors the one my students often use when they're only just grasping the concept I'm trying to teach them.

Neri's grin unfurls in a glorious sprawl across her beautiful face, and I lose my breath at the sight.

"That sounds exactly like what I'm in the mood for."

I place the book in her outstretched palm and then turn back to the leisure-reading shelf, so she doesn't see the triumphant smile stretching my mouth wide.

Is there a higher compliment than someone accepting your book recommendation?

I struggle to think of one.

Maybe if I wrote the book myself.

Wanting the high to continue, I scan the shelves. Unfortunately, the selection is relatively small. Most of the university's budget goes to academic texts, which, normally, I would agree is where the money should be spent. But right now, I just want to talk to Neri about genre fiction.

"I'm sorry Ramla doesn't have a better offering."

She lets out a gusty sigh, and I watch her shoulders fall from the corner of my eye. "I guess I shouldn't expect much. I'd be better off at a bookstore or public library. But I can't buy any more books until I have some organization in place for where to put them. And since Folk Haven doesn't have a library, RU is the closest option. But once I make it through these"—she hefts up her armful—"I'll make the drive to Toccoa and get a Georgia library card."

Lack of access to books is a struggle I can sympathize with.

"I understand your pain. I lived in Atlanta while earning my undergrad and New York City while earning my PhD. I glutted myself on visits to bookstores. Seemed those cities had one on every corner. And the libraries. Gods, those were gorgeous castles of knowledge." For a moment, I stare into space, mentally walking through the doors of the New York Public Library. There's not much I miss about living in big cities, but ready access to books is definitely one.

"I grew up down the street from a library." Neri's wistful voice brings my attention back to her. "I could walk to it. Never knew how lucky I was until my parents moved. They were so proud of how much bigger the new house was." She traces the figure of a badass woman handling a magical orb on the cover of the book that tops her pile. "I cried for a week straight. I mean, who cares about how many more guest rooms there were?" Her silver eyes find mine, a tenuous connection forming in the air between us. "I asked them if we could make one of the rooms into a library. Set up bookshelves on the walls and get some comfy chairs."

"Did they?" I ask my question hesitantly, almost fearful of the answer.

Suddenly, I can envision a younger version of the woman next to me, a little blonde girl with pigtails and hope in her sweet voice, clutching her armful of beloved stories, asking her parents to make a home for them.

Neri blinks, tearing her gaze from mine. When she clears her throat, as if having trouble speaking, I long to gather her in my arms and comfort her.

"They got me another bookshelf for my bedroom. They said an interior decorator would handle the rest of the house."

"Ridiculous," I mutter. "No house is complete without a library."

In that moment, I earn something precious.

A genuine Neri smile.

She used to give them to me all the time at the coffee shop. If I'd known there was an end to the supply, I would have worked hard to memorize the exact way they plumped her cheeks and caused her metallic eyes to shimmer.

I study her now. And I brainstorm how to inspire more happiness in her.

Well, if she wants a library, I can help her there.

"You should come over to my house. I have books."

Her mouth shifts, keeping half the curve as she smirks. "Is this you trying to pick me up? Because if I wasn't your anti-mate, offering me books would totally work."

A space deep in my gut clenches, part pain, part pleasure.

"I'm not. I swear. I just ..." How do I explain this need to be around her? To see joy on her face and know I helped put it there? This can't be some random manipulation from the gods. Even though I don't have words for this urge, I understand the reason it exists.

Because she's Neri.

"I would like to be friends."

13

———————

NERI

I'M HERE for the books.

That's the only possible reason I can fathom for accepting Seamus's invitation. Why else would I want to spend a moment in the presence of a mythic I so thoroughly dislike? It's certainly not because my nipples tightened when he fully absorbed my lesson on the romance genre.

I'm not here for him. Just for his literature.

Seamus's house sits off a road much closer to town than Sonya's does. I would have to cross two more bridges to get to her home. But if I think about the layout of Lake Galen from a bird's-eye view—a relatively easy thing for sirens to envision—traveling between Seamus's spot on the shoreline to Sonya's would take half the time if we went across the water.

Interesting how distances shift in that way in Folk Haven.

"Do all the selkies live around this cove?" I ask Seamus as we meet in front of my car.

The trees around his property stand tight together, blocking the view of any nearby neighbors. The road we turned off of continues on for a ways under a tunnel of branches.

"A few but not all. My parents are a short walk down the road. They own about half the land on this inlet."

"Really?" I think of the many siren houses that litter the banks of the stretch of water they claimed. From Sonya's dock, I can see at least five others. They all own smaller plots of land as opposed to large, stretching spaces.

"They aren't the only ones who live there. My siblings all have houses on the land. Sometimes, they refer to it as the MacNamara homestead," he explains.

"And there wasn't space for you on the sprawling MacNamara estate?" I follow him toward the front door of a simple yet sleek home with a modern feel. The structure can't be too old.

Seamus offers a smile over his shoulder as he slides a key into the front door. "There was, but I've always been the most introverted among my family. I liked the idea of being close but having my own place. When this property came up for sale, I grabbed it."

The property politics of Folk Haven interests me. From what Sonya has described, there's a division of territory related to type of mythics. But the town is a mixture. Restricting where humans can live in Folk Haven makes sense, but the mythic division confuses me.

But according to Sonya, that's how things have always been done, and there's not enough clamor to change it. Yet.

When we step inside, the first detail I notice is the bright glow of the space. Strategically placed windows let in the perfect amount of natural light. Seamus hasn't had to flip a switch, and I still see everything clearly.

"The library is this way." The selkie strolls down a hallway, not aware of how his words affect me.

"Library?" I jog after him. "I thought you said you just have some books."

He disappears around a corner.

"Seamus! Do you have a …"

Speech fails me as I step into a room crafted from a book-lover's fever dream.

Shelves. So many shelves. They stretch from floor to ceiling, and that ceiling rises almost an extra story above us.

Every inch of them is filled with books.

The only break in the beautiful display of spines occurs at the back wall of the room, but that space claims a different part of my heart. Wide windows provide an unobstructed view of Lake Galen. The blue-green water sprawls out, glittering in the afternoon sun as small waves play across the surface.

"Neri? Did you stop breathing?"

I gasp at Seamus's question, realizing that, yes, I did in fact forget to refill my lungs. But who needs oxygen when this room exists in the world? I might never need to consume another piece of food in my life, simply nourishing myself off of this vision.

"You live here?" I croak out.

"Yes. The previous owners of this land had an old cottage that would've cost a lot to fix up. I figured I'd be better spending my money on building my dream home." His shifting movement catches my eye, and I manage to tear my gaze away from everything else to focus on him. "Do you like it?"

"*Like* it?" The words moan from my soul. "I more than like it. I'm currently brainstorming how to blackmail you into handing over the deed to this house, so I can move in immediately. I'm sure you've done some shady shit in your life at some point." I step in close, holding up a threatening finger. "What did you do, Seamus MacNamara? Set a building on fire? Steal from a charity? Murder your enemy? Whatever it is, just hand over this house, and no one needs to find out."

My mock scowl falters under his wide-eyed smile. Suddenly, the selkie looks the perfect picture of innocence.

"Please, no. Anything but my dark, bloody past." All of a sudden, his warm hand wraps around the finger I was waving at him, and the gentle embrace freezes me in place. "You know, my friends are allowed to borrow books from this library whenever they want."

His skin burns hot against mine, sending heat through my body.

"I did not know that." My voice comes out quiet, almost like this man has hypnotized me with the promise of reading material.

He nods. "They're also welcome to hang out here." He waves with his free hand, gesturing to the entire glorious room.

Hang out? Sonya's house, filled to bursting with sirens, crosses my mind. "For parties?"

That earns me a grimace.

"No. Definitely not. Do you know how many drinks get spilled at parties?"

The selkie shudders, and I realize I must have a clean freak on my hands. I wouldn't say that's a bad thing. I've been known to get protective over the handling of my books.

"So, what does hanging out here mean?"

Seamus stares down at me for a moment, and his focus rests on my mouth, which reminds me how close we're standing. And that he's still holding my finger.

But then Seamus lets me go and turns his head, tilting his chin to indicate a particularly cushy couch.

"Hang out means, finding a good book and a comfy spot and reading. That's what I do most afternoons and evenings when I'm not teaching. And if I'm not teaching or reading, I tend to be grading." Seamus flicks his brown gaze to me and then away again, toward the shelves. He steps back, shoving his hands in his pockets during the retreat. "If you want to come by and borrow a book, you can. If you want to read it here, I never mind quiet company."

Quiet company. That sounds like perfection.

"I might take you up on that offer," I murmur as I forcibly forget the heat he aroused in my body and instead drift deeper into the room.

My path to the shelves takes me past a desk. Normally, the draw of so much reading material would hold my entire attention, but an image in the corner of my eye catches my notice. I pause to examine a pencil sketch lying atop open texts strewn across the desk surface.

The picture brings on a skittering of uncomfortable fear, as if a horde of spiders were racing down my spine. The lightly drawn lines show a creature, a bony, grotesque creation that doesn't look like anything I've ever heard of or read about. And I've read a lot of mythological texts after my mother refused to divulge more than the basics about our kind.

"What is that?" I finger the blank corner of the paper, my skin rebelling at the idea of coming into contact with even a rendering of whatever the terror is.

Could it be a monster? Is this why the stigma exists?

Seamus comes up beside me, a frown tugging at his lips as he realizes what I've found.

"It's ..." His voice drips with hesitation, and all my muscles clench in rebellion at the idea that someone else is denying me knowledge.

"Just tell me. I can handle it."

Seamus tries to run his fingers through his curly hair but seems to get stuck halfway into the gesture. With a grimace, he detangles himself, answering during the struggle. "The truth is, I don't know. I've been trying to figure it out."

Hand finally free, he gestures at the books. When I flip the closest one closed, I find one of the more respectable volumes discussing mythical creatures from around the world.

"Delta, my younger brother's mate, caught this thing trying to steal his selkie skin."

My hand flies to my mouth but isn't quick enough to stifle a gasp. Even I know how horrible an act the theft of a selkie's pelt is. "Did it get away?"

"Yes, but she wrestled the skin from it first. This was a few months ago. No one has seen it since. There's no record of a creature like it buying property here. The monster representative claims it's not one of his kind, although I don't think Moira believes him."

"Do you?" And I wonder who this representative is. *Have I met him without knowing his role in Folk Haven?*

Seamus stares out the large windows, as if the glittering view of Galen will provide all the answers.

"I do. Every interaction I've had with him, I ... well, I've had a good feeling. As if he's the decent sort." Seamus offers a rueful smile, shaking his head all the while. "That's an odd thing for me—to claim something without evidence. Maybe I shouldn't trust the monster's word." The selkie fingers the picture. "I've been attempting to find a record of a creature like this. I thought it might be one of the creations the gods formed on another continent. One we haven't seen in Folk Haven yet. But so far, my research hasn't proven fruitful."

"You're saying, an unknown, possibly dangerous entity is loose in the lake?" *Is that fear quivering my voice?*

Seamus's mouth tightens. "I don't know. Maybe. Selkies have taken more precautions when we wear our other forms. But the thing hasn't shown itself again. And it didn't attack Delta. Just tried to take something that didn't belong to it."

On a deep breath, the tension melts from his body.

"Lake Galen isn't that old, and every year, more magical beings arrive here. We can't know everything about this place. And other than looking creepy, this thing"—he taps the skeletal image—"hasn't attacked anyone. Black bears have done more harm than it has."

Seamus's conclusion doesn't put me entirely at ease, but I

let the matter drop for now and refocus on the library shelves, meandering away from the desk. I love how there's a mixture of beautifully bound hardbacks and spine-creased paperbacks. The well-used appearance gives me permission to reach for a title and slide it off the shelf.

The image on the cover, a cozy mystery with a cat on the front porch of a Victorian house, has me wanting to curl up in the closest chair and start reading.

A fantasy forms in my mind of a simple scene. Me, wrapped in a blanket, with a steaming cup of something to sip on, a well-worn book in my lap. And just over my shoulder, Seamus sitting at the mahogany desk by the windows, the dark wood a perfect reflection of his warm eyes. He'd have his head bent forward over student papers, pen scratching away as he doled out grades.

The imagined scene elicits a tight pressure in my chest. A need to release the uncomfortable weight forces out a short song I create with barely a thought.

> *In dreams I read beside you*
> *Could it be I misjudged you*

After the lyrics trail off, I relax, having allowed the truth into the air. A secret pleasure curls the corner of my lips, as I know he'll have forgotten the confession by now.

"I wish I could remember what you sing." The tone of Seamus's voice steals away my mischievous intent. There's no accusation or anger, like before.

He merely sounds wistful. And disappointed.

"I'm sorry," I mutter, sliding the book back on the shelf. "That's rude of me. Manipulating your memory. I'll stop."

I can hear my mother's horrified warnings whispering through my head. *"Never sing in public, Neri. Better yet, never sing at all. You're messing with peoples' minds, and they'll hurt you for it."*

As I blink away the sting of those harsh words, I find Seamus standing in front of me, his soft eyes wide with worry.

"Please don't stop. Sing whenever you want. I know your songs are for you, not me." He reaches for the book I almost took, slipping the paperback from its home and handing it over. "Besides, just because I don't remember them, it doesn't mean I don't know how beautiful you sounded."

Warm air fills my chest until I might burst with the whirlwind of emotions. To save myself, I fall back on a defense of teasing. "Maybe that's just what I *want* you to think. Ever consider that sirens all sound like toads? Croaking off-key songs to our hearts' content." I give his chest a playful poke. "Maybe that's why my ancestors went through all the trouble to make sure everyone in the world would forget."

Seamus grins down at me, and I have to fight the urge to kiss the dimple that dips in his left cheek. "Please croak away. My library is your pond. But I draw the line at eating flies."

The need to press my lips against his skin surges, and the only way I can keep my mouth to myself is by letting the pressure release in a simple rhyming tune.

You woo me with books
Tease me with looks

I would drink from your lips
Eased from the sips

Shock registers on the selkie's face as he processes my lyrics, but before he can act on them, I end the song. Seamus blinks once slowly and then faster, as if the rapid motion would replay the last minute in his mind.

But it won't.

Because as much as I find myself liking this man, I'm far from loving him. And the only beings who remember a siren's song other than our own kind are the ones who have earned a siren's heart.

Sonya's story brushes the back of my mind, a thought of that horrible sorcerer who thought he could steal access to our music.

The Collector's cruel nature meant he never stood a chance.

"See?" Seamus's question pulls me away from dark thoughts. He gazes down at me with dreaminess in his melted-chocolate gaze. "I don't recall one ribbit."

A pinch at my heart acts as a warning.

Because if I let this man, he might find a way to fully redeem himself.

But would that be so bad?

14

NERI

Seamus's library tempts me into staying much later than I should.

Something close to the scene I thought up ends up playing out—with me sitting on a couch by the windows and Seamus settling in at the desk. The few times I remember to look up from my book, he's typing out words on his computer, gaze flicking back and forth between the screen and a thick textbook open at his elbow. Because of the tantalizing view he makes, I'm quick to return to my reading.

Finally, when my stomach starts to protest, I pull a receipt from my back pocket to mark my page before climbing off the soft cushion. Stiff from sitting in the same position for a few hours, I reach my arms high over my head, letting out a satisfied groan as I hear my spine crack and experience the delicious tug of stretched muscles.

There's a series of coughs, and I glance over to see Seamus staring at the ground between us.

"Sorry. Didn't mean to interrupt you." I let my arms fall to my sides and then bend to grab my bag. "I'm going to head out."

"Already?" The selkie stands from his chair, blinking around the room, probably just as surprised as I am to realize the sun has dipped below the tree line outside the window.

"Believe me, I could read in this room until three in the morning and still regret having to go to bed." My stomach lets out another threatening grumble, and I shoot Seamus a rueful smile. "But a woman's gotta eat. Thanks for this." I hold up the half-finished mystery as I pass him by on my way to the front door.

"I have food," he declares before I make it across the room. "Plenty of it. I could make something. I need to eat too."

Immediate food is awfully tempting, which is how I find myself in the selkie's kitchen instead of driving back to Sonya's. My hunger is the reason I stay. That's it.

"This way, we can each have our own." Seamus places two naan in a warm cast iron skillet and then pulls out jarred pizza sauce and a bag of shredded mozzarella cheese.

I do my best not to watch the flex of biceps as he quickly slices a handful of mushrooms, a red pepper, and some fresh basil.

"Make yours however you want." He steps back from the offerings, and I build myself a personal pizza, heavy on the sauce and basil.

"This is a cute idea." With a flourish, I top everything off with a hearty pile of cheese.

"I'm nothing if not adorable," Seamus states in a deadpan voice that has me grinning. He makes up his own pizza, and he then slides the heavy cast iron pan into the preheated oven and sets a timer.

Then, we wait.

"How about a drink? I have water and wine."

"How biblical of you," I tease. "Wine if it's red, please."

Seamus pulls a bottle of Chianti from a cabinet and fills up two glasses before handing me one. The glass feels delicate under my fingers, and I have to admit, it's nice, spending time with a man who has his life together enough to keep a good house. No overly full trash can or the lingering scent of Cool Ranch Doritos.

I did more dating in my early twenties, where hygiene and cutlery were not guaranteed.

Then, I met Ronald.

Or more like, he was presented to me.

Just the thought of that relationship has me cringing.

"You don't like the wine?" Seamus asks, misinterpreting my expression. He opens a cabinet and pulls out another bottle, ready to replace my drink in an instant.

"No! It's not that. The wine is great." I take a sip and enjoy the dry, fruity flavor. After I swallow, I give him a thumbs-up. "Tasty. I was just thinking about something unpleasant for a second."

"Me?" He settles against the counter across from where I stand, and we hold stares.

"Surprisingly, no. After today and all this book bribery, I'm going to have a hard time thinking of you as unpleasant. But don't take that as a challenge." My glare lacks fire, and I'm charmed to watch him blush in response.

Damn The Winged One's tricks. How am I letting this selkie win me over?

Needing to focus on something else, I force my gaze to my drink. My next sip reveals a totally new flavor that has me staring harder at the red liquid.

Is this some shapeshifting wine?

All of a sudden, my taste buds detect strong smoky notes. I take a larger gulp and realize the flavor isn't on my tongue but sits inside my nose.

That's when I see the flames through the oven window.

"Seamus!" His name yelps out of my mouth, sending the man jumping. "Fire!"

The selkie follows my pointing finger to the oven, and then for some reason, he decides to open the door. Flames stretch out, reaching over the lip of the oven, as if searching for more fuel to burn.

When the professor freezes at the sight, I give up on him making smart decisions. I leap into action, ripping open the cabinet under the sink and finding a small fire extinguisher. You don't work in a restaurant for a decade and not know where to look for safety equipment.

"Move," I bark at Seamus, and he stumbles back.

With steady hands, I aim the hose and press the release, thanking the gods the canister hasn't expired as it lets out a cloud of white foam. The substance immediately douses the tiny inferno, leaving a chemical smell behind.

Finally doing something helpful, Seamus reaches out shaking fingers to turn off the oven.

The kitchen falls quiet, except for our panting breaths. Adrenaline still courses through my veins, offering a sense of euphoria. I grin at Seamus, expecting him to laugh or thank me or maybe apologize.

Instead, I gaze into a face filled with panic.

This isn't the first time the selkie has looked at me this way. The other was right after I got that cookie chunk out of his lungs.

Of course. He thinks I saved him.

That would be his first conclusion. The horror on his face sparks my temper.

"No," I growl at the selkie I just began to like, aiming the fire extinguisher his way. "It was a small kitchen fire. Not some life-saving event. Keep your shit on lock because if you turn into an asshole again, I swear to The Winged One, I will spray you with this."

Seamus holds his hands up, and I watch as he tucks away his wild reaction. But even as his face clears, my annoyance remains. The extinguisher lets out a clank when I set it down on the granite countertop.

There's no food, and a guy who claimed we could be friends is still reacting like I'm trying to rope him into an unwanted marriage.

"What's your problem anyway?" I round on Seamus, finding him staring into his foam-filled oven.

"Sorry?"

Fully immersed in my hangry stage now, I'm officially done with his jittery bullshit. "Why are you so hung up on this selkie mating myth? You'd better give me some kind of reason." I snatch up my wine and throw back the rest, ready to storm out of this beautiful house because I'm done with toxic relationships. "If you don't tell me, we're done. No friendship. No nothing."

I'm already stepping toward the door when his ragged voice stops me.

"Wait, Neri. Please. I'll tell you."

15

———

SEAMUS

Neri's glare holds a heat that could rival the flames she just put out. I'm still reeling over her quick thinking. And also that she was so close to a dangerous situation.

One that I'd put her in.

I see the cause of the fire now that the inferno is contained. The cloth holder I used to grip the cast iron's hot handle sits, smoldering, half-charred away. Apparently, I forgot to take the holder out before closing the oven door.

I'm the cause of the fire.

And that's the reason panic pummeled my chest a moment ago. My carelessness could have hurt Neri. It wasn't until her threat to extinguish me that I realized there was another way to interpret this situation.

Not that I can blame her for expecting the worst from me. And now, she wants answers. Ones she deserves after the horrible way I treated her.

"I'll tell you," I repeat. "But let me make you a sandwich. A cold one. Hopefully, I can't mess that up."

The siren keeps her hard expression in place but gives a short nod. As I pull out the bread, cheese, and cold cuts, I start talking.

"There was a girl in high school I had a huge crush on. Ginger Thompson. She was a selkie and the same age as me, and we had a few classes together. We'd study together and get food sometimes, and I thought she might like me too. So, I asked her to homecoming." I arrange all the sandwich fixings on the table in front of Neri, letting her build one first. "She said yes."

The siren raises a single eyebrow, but she doesn't interrupt, letting me tell my story as she piles cheese on her slices of bread.

"I was excited. First official date, and I wanted to do it right. Got my hair cut and bought a nice shirt. Got her flowers. My parents agreed to let me take their new truck. I thought the night would be amazing. Then, the day before the dance, she canceled on me."

Despite maintaining an air of anger, Neri offers a sympathetic grimace before biting into her food.

"Ginger told me she tripped at the top of the bleachers and would've taken a bad tumble. Only she was *rescued*." The word twists on my tongue like a curse. "By Lenny Powel. And you know the lore. A selkie will know their mate when they save them from great danger. Naturally, that meant our human classmate Lenny was her fated mate. That they were meant to be together. She told me all of this like I'd be happy for her. Lenny took her to the dance. I stayed home and read a book."

Gods, I sound pathetic. And I kind of was with my teenage broken heart.

"That was a dick move on her part," Neri offers after she swallows. "But are you really telling me you have this irrational reaction to the idea just because of one high school girl?"

"No." I clear my throat. "Well, not exactly. Not how you're

saying. The canceled date sucked, but it didn't make me hate the myth. It was everything that came afterward."

My own hunger makes itself known with a sharp jab to my gut, so I throw together a sandwich for myself.

"Ginger and Lenny started officially dating. I kept my distance for a while. Not wanting to bask in their lovey-dovey stuff. But time went by, and I got over my crush and started missing my friend. That was what Ginger and I had been before the whole homecoming thing. Friends. When I stopped pouting, reached out, and started talking to her again, we got along fine. Except for one thing."

The memories that creep in are a sickness in the back of my brain, sparking the fury that's never truly gone away.

"What's the thing?" Neri stares at me over her wineglass as she sips.

As my anger has grown, hers seems to have waned with the story.

I make a note to myself: *Sirens likes stories.*

"Lenny Powel."

"You were still jealous?"

"No. I was pissed off. The guy was a jerk, treated my friend like a doormat, and she refused to entertain the idea of breaking up with him."

Neri's eyebrows creep up. "Seriously? She was that dialed in to the lore?"

My nod comes jerky. "Some parents teach that stuff to their kids like it's gospel. Like the gods at some point ordained that a selkie *must* mate the person who rescues them."

I take an angry bite of my sandwich, not tasting a thing even though I slathered Dijon mustard on both pieces of bread. Unfortunately, I took too big of a bite, so my furious chewing goes on for a long time, and I start to worry I might choke again if I try swallowing the mass.

Neri, more perceptive than she ought to be, rolls her eyes

while the corner of her mouth tilts up. Taking pity on me, she opens a couple of cabinets until she finds a glass and fills it at the faucet before handing the drink over. I swallow down the cool liquid and my sandwich clog, wincing as my throat stretches around the invasion.

"What happened?" Neri gets her own glass of water before scooping up her plate and coming around to my side of the counter. Standing closer to me, all signs of her annoyance gone.

"We remained friends. She stayed with him. All through high school and college and then years after that. They fought all the time, and whenever I brought it up, she'd just shrug. Like she thought that must be normal. Or that the gods required it of her."

"Are they still together?"

"No, thank The Finned One. I think it was him cheating that did it. Selkie mates don't cheat. Not ever. Ginger didn't give me the details, but she'd ended things. Problem was that the whole mind-set fucked with her. She'd spent years building her life around an asshole because she thought their partnership was a fated plan."

My sandwich doesn't seem appealing anymore as I remember how the light drained out of Ginger over the years until she was a faded shell of herself. She had given everything to that guy, and it was never enough.

"Where is she now?"

"Last we talked, about a month ago, she was in Seattle, working as a schoolteacher. Lenny lives in Atlanta, and I think she just wanted to be as far from him as possible."

At least Ginger smiled more the last time we talked. And from the way she sighed over another teacher at her school, I thought maybe she hadn't given up completely on the idea of romance. Glad to know Lenny hadn't stolen all of that hope from her.

"I'm sorry." Neri's sad voice pulls my focus to her.

"For what? Ginger is the one who got screwed over, not me." Heat rushes into my cheeks as I replay my interactions with Neri again. "I had no reason to treat you the way I did."

"Agreed." The siren abandons her water and goes back to wine. "But I'm sorry I assumed you didn't have valid reasons to dislike the mythology around your kind. Doesn't let you off the hook for yelling at me, but I get why the idea might make you panicky."

Silence flows between us, but the air isn't heavy with it. Instead, we both, in unspoken agreement, return to eating. And the kitchen transforms around me. The room itself doesn't change, but the comfort increases tenfold.

Because I'm here with Neri.

Without facing her, I absorb all I can about her presence. The warmth emanating from her body just beside mine, the subtle scent of rain on the wind that clings to her hair, and the quiet, content hum she lets out after every bite. Not enough of a song to make me forget.

I want her to sing again, but at the same time, I don't because I hate the idea of missing any moment with the siren. She's intelligent and weird, and she conveys knowledge with skill, keeping me on the edge in the best kind of way. Her short blonde hair, now free of her baseball hat and ponytail, brushes her cheeks, teasing me to tuck the strands away for a better look. I want to fondle the spun silk, but I hold myself back.

That's all I ever do around Neri. Hold myself back.

Sometimes, I forcefully push myself away from her. All out of fear of the idea of the selkie mating myth. Like I'll be trapped in her rescuing clutches and lose all sense of myself. Like I'll mate with a complete stranger who will work for my misery on a daily basis.

Neri would never do that.

The thought hits me so hard that I grab on to the counter to keep from falling off my stool.

Neri might have a sharp temper, but she's kind. And funny. And smart. And beautiful. I'm wildly attracted to her, and I know exactly why. This isn't some mysterious force sent from the gods, and it's not a teaching that my parents brainwashed me with from childhood.

I want her, for her.

"I'm glad you're still friends with Ginger." Neri's declaration barely pierces my turmoil of self-discovery, and I work to focus on her words.

"You are?"

She nods. "Lots of guys would have jumped on the chance to insult her or be angry with her forever because she made one selfish choice when she was a teenager. But you got over it. And you kept supporting her, even when she made decisions you didn't like. Some guys try to fix women. I'm not saying that she should have stayed in that toxic relationship. But I think you did the best you could—by supporting her as she figured her own life out."

I blink my surprise as Neri names all the urges I fought against these past years. The ones I knew I had to set aside if I wanted to keep my friend. The ones that fueled my unhealthy reaction to Neri's kind act.

"You're a good friend." Her silver irises gleam as she stares up at me. "And I'm glad we're friends now too."

Friendship, normally a wonderful thing, is a pale descriptor of the connection I want to form with this siren.

Moira was right. I screwed myself out of a relationship with an amazing woman because of my irrational hang-ups.

Gods-damn it. What am I going to do now?

16
———

NERI

I TRY NOT to squirm when Seamus smiles at me the moment he walks through the doors of Coffee & Claws. After weeks of spending time in his library, I should be comfortable around him. We have a routine, where the selkie will text me if he's at home, and if I'm free and in a reading mood—which let's be honest, I'm always in a reading mood—I'll head over and sink into a good book. Seamus usually works at his desk or finds a book for himself and reads on another couch across from the one I've claimed as mine. We don't exchange many words, but in that space, the silence doesn't weigh heavy. Everything fits.

Outside of the library is where I run into a major problem. My friends, like Heath and Moira and the sirens I'm getting to know, smile at me whenever we see each other. But when Seamus curls his lips in greeting, the innocent gesture sets off strange dips and swoops inside my body. Like gravity has decided to toss around my organs for fun. A feeling more likely to occur during flight.

Or at least, I think the sensations are similar. I haven't flown since I was very young. I barely remember the freedom or the sensation of soaring anymore.

Which is why the smile of a selkie causing flight-like weightlessness is so disconcerting.

"The usual?" I ask once Seamus makes his way to the counter.

The question itself elicits another positive swoop that has nothing to do with Seamus and everything to do with me knowing someone in this town well enough to have identified their usual. I don't want to work the front counter of Coffee & Claws forever, but every day, I'm surer Folk Haven is my kind of town. A place where I want to know people and want them to know me.

Just maybe not as a barista. Still, I haven't figured out what I *do* want to be known as, so purveyor of warm beverages works for now.

"Yes, please. And"—Seamus leans in, his advance prompting me to mirror the move without thought until there are mere inches separating us—"I believe I'll be dangerous today. A peanut butter cookie?"

I narrow my eyes, attempting my best glare, but the corners of my mouth twitch. "Should I crumble it up, so you can carefully consume it with a spoon?"

He snorts, his lips parting to show a set of pearly-white teeth. There's a barely noticeable gap between the front two, and I find myself homing in on the little space.

What would it be like to slip my tongue along that minuscule gap? Would his tongue stretch out to meet mine?

"How much do I owe you?"

Every part of my body has the swoops again, and I find I need to stare very hard at the cash register to figure out the simple addition.

We're friends, I remind myself.

"Three forty-nine." I'm impressed with how not breathless my answer is.

Seamus hands over a five. "Keep the change."

Then, his dimple appears. Under the hint of a five o'clock shadow.

When did he start growing a beard?

Twice, I almost spill boiling hot water on my hand because I'm contemplating how facial hair would feel, rubbing against my skin.

What is the matter with me?

I used to manage a busy restaurant so well that my parents wanted me to take over the venture completely. Every night, I juggled fifty tasks and fended off advances from handsy customers without stumbling over inappropriate fantasies. Of course, I was also miserable in that fast-paced environment and didn't have anything joyful in my life to daydream about other than leaving everything behind.

Sorry, not sorry, Ronald.

But now, I feel like I've reverted back to my teenage brain. Mooning over a man while ignoring the fact that I have no life plan.

After sucking in a deep breath and using the extra oxygen to calm all the random flutters in my body, I turn to the counter to hand over Seamus's tea and cookie.

But he's not there.

He didn't leave though. Leaning past the espresso machine, I realize the selkie set himself up at one of the small round tables near the window. His laptop is out and everything.

Which of The Winged One's tricks is this?

"Are you staying here?" I baldly ask, approaching his table with a to-go cup and wrapped cookie in my hand.

"Yes. Sorry, I should've said. I guess this is not exactly my usual today. But I don't mind drinking out of the disposable cup instead of a mug." Seamus rearranges his items to make room on the table for his order.

With an overwhelming sense of trepidation, I place his order next to his computer. "Why are you working here? You never work here." I try out a smile that's more like a grimace and a laugh that sounds too stiff. "Is this a joke?"

Seamus's thick brown brows dip. "No. The semester is over, so I don't need to be on campus. But I have research I'm doing over the summer break, and people like working in coffee shops. Thought I might try it out."

"But"—I struggle for a reason to get him out of this chair and out of my eyeline—"it can get loud in here." The relative emptiness of the shop at the moment isn't helping my case.

Seamus glances around and then gestures at another regular sitting across the way. "Delta works here all the time and doesn't seem to mind."

"You know Delta?" The question is out before I remember the info Sonya gave me a few weeks ago.

"She's mated to my brother Calder. And I've been trying to convince her to apply for a position at Ramla University," he explains.

"Of course." *Maybe if I put his drink outside of the shop, he'll follow me, and then I can dive inside and lock the doors before he turns around.*

I know I'm being a horrible friend, plotting for ways to get rid of the selkie, but I'm worried what erotic, unwanted trains of thought I might get caught on if I'm in his presence for too long without the distraction of a book.

Seamus tilts his head toward the other professor. "We're not so different. Do you try to shoo Delta out when she works here?"

"No!" I glare down at his inquisitive face and then remind myself not to scowl at customers. Or friends. "I'm not trying to kick you out. I was just ... surprised. And you're right. You're *no* different than Delta. Enjoy your tea." As I walk away, I keep my pace steady and not-at-all jerky. But I'm off-kilter with this selkie around.

The problem is, his confession. Now, I know Seamus is not a complete jerk but instead someone who watched a person close to him hurting for years. He lashed out to protect himself, and now, the only reason I can find to be mad at him is that he makes me feel things I don't want to feel.

Things I don't even want to name.

He's going to be here, where I work, for who knows how long?

I have to be at the café for the next four hours to finish my shift.

He won't stay that long. Will he?

17

———

SEAMUS

I believe my research is paying off.

My goal: persuade Neri to see me as a desirable male she might consider going on a date with.

A few months ago, I overheard my teaching assistant saying a term I'd never heard before.

Thirst trap.

Thinking she was referring to some kind of water-quality topic I wasn't acquainted with, I asked her to define the word for me, not understanding why the question caused her to blush so hard.

Then, she did as asked, and I realized why.

Thirst traps have nothing to do with water-quality management.

They have everything to do with how I plan on wooing Neri Onassis.

I let the definition of *thirst trap* drift to a far-removed part of my brain I rarely sifted through until I realized how largely I'd screwed up my chance to be with an amazing woman. When considering how best to place myself before her as a viable romantic candidate, the concept of thirst trap reemerged.

I researched the term, diving deep into what constituted a highly rated thirst trap.

The qualities I compiled that seemed related to my natural state included wearing a flannel shirt with rolled-up sleeves, allowing my beard to grow in enough that a dark shadow engulfed my jaw, letting my brown curls fall in a messy array around my face, and taking as many opportunities as presented to display my muscles.

I don't have too many of those last ones, but I've been told my shoulders are relatively broad.

With every ounce of my concentration, I try to appear unaware of myself as I stretch my arms and shoulders, rolling them under the fabric of my button-up so the material stretches over the expanse. After the display, I scratch my five o'clock shadow and throw a covert glance to the side.

Neri lingers at the counter, wiping the surface down with a damp rag.

The same thing she's been doing since she served the last customer five minutes ago.

Is she watching me?

I have no definitive proof. Also, this shirt is getting overly warm. Flannel and June in Georgia do not mix.

An idea presents itself, and I act on it before talking myself out of the move. With a put-upon casual air, I rise from my chair. Then, at a slow pace that I hope conveys a sense of disinterest, I start unbuttoning my shirt.

At the third button, I hear a clatter and look up in time to see Neri scrambling to pick up a scattering of pens that tumbled over her counter, no doubt housed a moment ago in the toppled-over cup that now rolls onto the floor. With a few long strides, I reach the register, bending down to scoop up the container and offering it to her.

"Thanks," she mutters.

"No problem. Everything okay?" I rest my hands on the surface between us, putting my bare forearms on display.

"Yes," she clips the word off and then sighs as her steely eyes meet mine.

Her soft lips part to say something else, and I lean forward to make sure I hear every syllable, my focus on her mouth.

Suddenly, the world tilts around me, and I have to grip the counter edge to keep from staggering. As the dizziness dissipates, I realize what happened.

"You sang at me." My eagerness colors my voice, and Neri stares down at her pens as she carefully arranges them.

"Did I?"

I'm still grinning when I make my way back to my table. My flannel hangs half-open, revealing the white T-shirt underneath. Before sitting down, I decide to continue the disrobing.

Just as I finger the next button, disaster strikes.

My brothers walk in.

Owen's jubilant presence fills the café before he says a word. There's just something about the way the guy smiles at the whole room and swaggers across the floor. My gaze flicks to Neri, and I try not to grimace at the welcoming expression she offers my sibling. Meanwhile, Calder veers off to drop a kiss on his mate's forehead. Delta hooks a finger in the collar of his polo shirt, tugging him down to whisper something in his ear.

Both of them glance my way, and I hurriedly drop into my seat, tugging my flannel the rest of the way off with efficient movements.

No more striptease when my annoying younger siblings are around.

"Is that my dusty, old professor brother I see there?" Owen's voice booms across the small space, and I suddenly understand Neri's warning about the volume in this place. But I bet she didn't predict all the noise would come from one overly exuberant selkie.

I sink lower into the tiny chair, as if the spindly back will hide me from view.

Owen doesn't take the hint located in my hunched shoulders. Instead, he plops down in the chair across from mine. The empty space I hoped Neri might fill whenever she got her break.

"I'm working," I growl.

My brother gives me his dopiest smile. He's good at those. "Oh, really?"

"Yeah, really," Calder declares, pulling a chair up to my table that's barely big enough for one. "Delta says he's been working really hard, trying to catch the attention of the barista."

I grit my teeth and glare across the café at my brother's mate. The dragon's purple eyes hide behind a large set of glasses, but I still spy the hint of mischief in them when she smirks at me.

Traitor, I mouth.

The woman's grin plumps her cheeks as she reaches down to pet the head of her strange-looking dog. The thing peers out of the top of its carrier, gazing around the room with bug eyes. I'd rather be talking to the constantly anxious creature than these two buffoons.

"This is good." Owen claps a hand on my shoulder, as if he thinks I need encouragement. "Glad to see you going for it."

"I'm not going anywhere." The words are a pathetic response, but I can't concentrate when the perfect woman is twenty feet from me and my brothers are threatening to ruin my already-precarious position.

"Of course you are. Into the dating world!" Owen thrusts his fist into the air, and I half-expect a *huzzah* for emphasis.

"I've dated before," I growl at him, not wanting Neri to overhear and think I went monk after the high school rejection. I meant what I said about getting over my crush on Ginger.

Owen scoffs. "You call those dates? I call them business meetings."

"They were … wait. How would you know what my dates were like?"

The asshole breaks off a bite of my cookie and pops it in his mouth. Of course, he swallows it just fine, shrugging as he does. "I get bored. So, I spy on you. It's not hard. You always take them to the same restaurant. Not that Folk Haven has a lot of choices, but still."

"Are you kidding me?"

"Careful," Calder warns, his eyes on Owen. "If you get him too riled, he'll storm out." My baby brother's lips tighten as he fights a smirk.

"That's true. Seamus does love an angry, dramatic exit. I blame all those soap operas he and Mama used to watch." Owen turns to acknowledge me, as if I haven't been beside him this whole time. "Don't get your boxers in a bunch and huff off. I swear, I just want to help."

"My underwear is completely orderly." My comeback falls like a whale without a parachute in the middle of the table, and I watch my brothers exchange a look, both of them mashing their mouths closed, likely to keep from laughing.

And I refuse to admit I was contemplating scooping up my belongings and stomping out of the café in righteous glory a moment before they identified it as my MO.

There is nothing worse in the world than when a sibling gets to say *I told you so.*

I would rather set my diplomas on fire than give them the opportunity.

"Okay," Owen chokes out and then clears his throat. "Okay. Back on topic. Winning yourself a siren. What have you done so far?"

"I—what? Nothing. Absolutely—I wouldn't." If I ever stumble this badly over my words in front of a classroom, I'd dismiss the group for the day. Struggling for a coherent sentence, I land on a factual one. "She gets me tea and cookies."

And now, I sound like a toddler.

There's a warm press of a palm against my forehead, and I belatedly smack Calder's hand away.

"What are you doing?"

"Checking if you have a fever." My youngest brother watches me with confused amusement. "You usually make more sense than this."

Owen knocks his knuckles hard on the table, as if that'd somehow give him ultimate power over this ambush. "Never mind. The problem is, we're asking him to talk. Let me just give you some pointers instead. No responses or thanks necessary. But feel free to send a fruit basket to my office. I'm a fan of cantaloupe." The arrogant selkie, who I'm not sure has ever made sense in all the decades I've grown up with him, leans back and scans me with his eyes.

And I try not to sit straighter in my chair as he does so.

"Good outfit choice. Casual but not stained or wrinkled. I think the beard is working for you. Not all patchy, like this fucker's." Owen taps a fist against Calder's shoulder, and the youngest of us merely grins back, not fazed by the teasing.

I could probably learn something from him.

Owen snaps his fingers, like that's the switch flipping on his lightbulb of genius. "Your ass."

"I'm not an ass!" Luckily, I had enough forethought to lean forward and whisper the rebuke rather than shouting it loud enough for the whole café to hear.

Delta probably would've found the announcement entertaining.

Neri might have contradicted me.

"I meant, your ass, as in your butt. You need to show it off."

There's some comfort that Calder is also looking at Owen as if his words had turned into gibberish.

"I have not, nor will I ever, moon a woman to garner her romantic interest," I whisper furiously. "First off, it's rude. Likely sexual harassment. And second, what kind of person would even go for that?"

"Yes. Who *would* go for that?" Owen's expression turns contemplative, but then he shakes his head. "Off topic. I'm not saying you drop your drawers and try to blind her with your undercooked sourdough loaves."

Calder buries his face in his hands, and I wonder if those strange noises he's making mean he's crying. Who knows? I might start sobbing if I have to keep suffering through this conversation.

"Owen! Calder!" Neri's melodic voice calls out my brothers' names, and I glance over in time to watch the gorgeous siren set two to-go cups on the counter. When she catches me looking, the entrancing woman offers a friendly smile.

Such a lovely smile. As if I were a favorite book she just noticed on the shelf. If only Neri would spend hours focused on me the way she pores over new reading material.

"Seamus. Pay attention."

I tear my eyes away from Neri and find Owen leaning toward me, acting like he has important wisdom to impart.

"People want to know a guy has some junk in the trunk. All you've gotta do is bend over, like you're picking something up. Let your fitted jeans do the rest of the work."

"I will do no such thing!" The phrase and tone I say the words in suddenly remind me of when Moira asked Grandma MacNamara if she wanted to go see *Magic Mike*. Both of us were equally scandalized by the mere idea.

Owen stands and accepts the coffee Calder went to grab for him. "I'm just trying to help you out. I mean, really, of the four of us, who has the most game?"

I glance between my brothers and ponder my sister. "Calder is the only one with a partner," I conclude.

Owen snorts and then leans around our brother to peer across the café. "Delta!"

The dark-haired woman looks up from her laptop. "Huh?"

"How much game does Calder have?"

The dragon glances at her mate, and my youngest brother wears a besotted grin as he gazes back.

"Zero." But she smiles with a kind of exasperated love that tells everyone in the room he didn't need any.

"I rest my case." Owen hooks his arm around Calder's neck. "Now, let's get out of here before you get your woman pregnant with that inappropriate staring you're doing."

Calder chuckles and waves at his love as Owen tows him out of the café. Delta goes back to her work, and I resume pretending to know what's on my computer screen. The thing is dark, in power-save mode from inactivity. I swipe my finger on the touchpad a few times to wake it back up, trying to ignore the memory of Owen's voice as I type in my password.

"Your ass ... you need to show it off."

As I struggle not to shoot an obvious look toward Neri, I can't help my fingers tapping out an agitated rhythm.

Oh no, look at that. I knocked my pen off the table.

I bend in my chair to scoop it up. *Damn, can't believe I'm so clumsy, kicking it out of reach like that.*

The thing is a slipping hazard. I scan the area, making sure no one is in immediate danger of face-planting by stepping on my writing material.

Nope. Everyone is safely seated. And Neri is tucked behind the register, wiping the counter with that rag. Again.

With excessive casualness, I rise from my chair, step toward my pen, make sure to face away from the counter ... and bend over.

18

———————

NERI

IF I HAVE ENOUGH mental energy to contemplate a man's ass for half my work shift, then I need a new job.

So, it's Seamus MacNamara's butt that has me walking into Folk Haven Realty for an appointment with Moira MacNamara after a few days of dealing with the torment. No need to inform her that her brother's behind spurred this interest in a career change.

"Hi, Neri. Come on back to my office." The selkie waves me through a wide doorway, revealing a sleek office layout that's modern and colorful with a glass-topped desk and upholstered chairs with bold patterns.

"How's life treating you in Folk Haven? Think your move here might be permanent?" Moira settles behind her desk, waving me to one of the plush chairs. The cushions cradle me perfectly, and I can see how buyers would relax in this office as Moira guided them through the search for a new home.

"Life is better than it was before Folk Haven, so no

complaints. I think I'd like to stay here, but ..." My response trails off as I search for an answer that fits.

But that's just it. I'm not sure *I* fit.

"This is a tight-knit community." Moira twirls a pen between her fingers. "I imagine, for a newcomer, it can be a struggle to figure out how to be a part of it."

Relief suffuses my body and lightens a weight I didn't realize tugged down the middle of my brow. "Yes. That's a big part of it. Things would be easier if I knew what I wanted to do with my life in general. Then, I could find that here. But I'm just drifting right now. Don't know which dock is the right one for me."

If anyone is going to get a boating metaphor, it'll be the selkie who lives on a lake.

Moira nods, offering me a genuine smile as she leans forward, elbows braced on her desk. "Let's talk then and see if this might be your dock. Know anything about real estate?"

"Some about commercial. My parents own multiple restaurants, and I helped them find the location for the newest one. Also, the highest-performing one." At least, it was before I left. I've avoided conversations with the two of them, much less looked up how the restaurant is doing under new management.

"Restaurant to café? Sure you don't want to be in the food industry?" Moira's thick brown brow curves up with her question.

My hair falls in a curtain over my face when I shake my head so hard. Pushing the strands away, I meet her eyes, trying not to think how they're the same shade as her brother's. "No. Gods, no. The café is fine for now, mainly because Sonya and Heath never keep it open later than eight. I am not a night owl. My bedtime, when I get to choose it, is ten p.m. At the latest."

Moira snorts. "You sound like Seamus. He instituted a quiet-hour curfew when we were growing up."

Damn. That makes me like him more, and I'm already above the proper amount. "Smart man."

"I wasn't trying to set you two up the other day. Just in case that wasn't clear." Moira lets her shoulders rest back against the mesh of her ergonomic chair. "I was curious. I like to be in the know."

"Sirens like to be in the know too," I offer.

"True. But I've run into plenty of secretive sirens. If you can't remember the songs, you don't get the stories and all that." Moira's smile loses some of the ease it held before, but I don't think she's mad. Maybe just annoyed that she doesn't get to have every piece of information. "Still, if you want to keep your fingers on the pulse of Folk Haven, working in my office will do that for you. No one moves to this town without me knowing about it."

My head tilts in disbelief, and she corrects herself with a grimace.

"No one buys a house without me knowing. There are cases like yours, of relatives moving in with owners. And what's a town without a squatter or two? But there's an art to buying and selling real estate in this area. I'm sure you can imagine."

"Because so many mythics live here?" I guess.

Moira nods. "The market in town is easier to deal with. No restrictions on who can buy where. Mythics and humans all intermingle. But the lake? That's the tricky bitch."

"How so?"

The woman's shrewd eyes track over my face, as if she's trying to read my thoughts before I speak them. "Because of the boundaries. Are you aware of the divides?"

"Sonya tried to explain. You mean, like how most of the sirens live in one cove?"

"That cove exists within a larger territory. The Winged One's territory."

"What does that mean?"

Moira drums her fingers once and then stands in a fluid motion, waving for me to follow her. We head back out to the sitting room, which is just as comfortable and stylish as her back office. The selkie moves to the front doors, but instead of exiting, she turns the lock and flips a wooden sign, designating her office as closed. Then, she settles on the plush emerald couch and gestures for me to join her. That's when I notice the coffee table is not just a simple piece of wooden furniture.

The surface displays a map of Lake Galen.

"How much do you know about the history of the lake?"

After Galen's song, I know a lot more than I did before. "Sonya sang me the story of The Collector. And how the lake was made to cleanse his toxic magic from the area."

Moira nods. "Lake Galen was made by mythics. A group worked together, and then each claimed a piece of the resulting body of water. They all shared a hope that more of our kind would move here, and they worked to make the area ready. Here"—she points to the southeast portion of the map—"is Folk Haven. They decided the town they built and the part of the lake closest to it would be neutral territory. I believe they knew not everything could be predicted about the future of people living here." Her finger tracks along the eastern branch of the lake. "This is the area where we sell houses to anyone, including humans."

"Why?"

At my question, Moira meets my gaze. "A few reasons. One, the lake is too large to hide from them. You'd need hundreds of witches, all with protective abilities, to shield everything. We don't even have a hundred witches, period. But the ones we do have live here." She draws her finger farther up the lake's right branch. "Most don't even bother warding their own homes, as far as I'm aware. And when you don't hide from humans, they find you. There are just too many. Maybe if we lived in the middle of the Amazon rain forest but not in Georgia." Moira's wry smile speaks of acceptance of the inevitable.

"You said there's another reason? I mean, just because they can find Folk Haven doesn't mean you have to sell them property, right?"

"True. But that would raise suspicion. Plus, there's an important reason to want humans around." The woman's businesslike nature cracks with a playful wiggle of her eyebrows. "Mates."

"Ah." That makes sense.

"Yes. Folk Haven is more than just a safe place for mythics. The founders always wanted this to be a place where we could thrive. And we need future generations to do that since most of us aren't immortal."

"Most of us?" I squeak out the question. "There are immortal mythics?"

Moira gives me a funny look. "I'm not trying to be insulting, but did your parents share anything about our kind with you?"

I shrug. "Not really. My dad is human, and my mom thought blending in was the best course since sirens don't have to sing or extend our wings. She always told me I should pretend to be normal."

"That's not normal." Moira scowls. "That's *ordinary*. You being who you are is normal. Everyone has a different version, so no one is wrong."

A glow infuses my chest, and I try not to smile too broadly. "We allow humans to live in Folk Haven to broaden the dating pool?"

The annoyance leaves Moira's face with a snort. "We don't only sell to singles ready to mingle, but yes. We realize that our kind need a human population to survive. Supporting businesses is important too."

"You keep saying *we*. Are there more people who work in your office?"

"I had a part-time assistant for a stretch, but when I say *we*, I mean, The Council. A governing body that oversees the health and safety of the mythics in Folk Haven and on Lake Galen. There is an elected representative for each of the factions that live in the area. Witches. Of the Fin"—she points to the widest section of the lake—"Of the Wing"—the middle branch of Lake Galen and where Sonya's home sits—"Of the Claw"—up the left branch. Then, with a grim smile, she waves at the farthest section of the northwest, at the edge of the map. "Here, lie monsters."

"So, The Council has a representative for witches, wings, fins, claws, and monsters. What about mythics formed from the hands of other gods? The Hard One? The Cold One? And The Hot One?" I at least know my basic gods even though my mother never spent any time praying to them.

Legends tell that a powerful being from another world—or another dimension depending on who is relating the story— discovered Earth thousands of years ago. They are called The Dark One. The Dark One had offspring, and they gifted Earth to their children: The Winged One, The Finned One, The Clawed One, The Hard One, The Cold One, and The Hot One. They became gods in this world, and they had their fun among the primitive humans. At one point the gods started forming creatures of their own to live in this world. Mythics. Some say the gods grew bored of Earth and left. Some say The Dark One commanded they cease interfering. Others claim the gods still walk among us.

Whatever the truth, I find it strange a mythic community would only grant space to some of the gods creations.

"A few mythics of those designations live in the town. But only a handful. The Council represents the founders and the largest populations."

Doesn't seem fair to me, the lack of representation. But I keep my mouth shut, still not sure if this is an interview.

But if it is, do I want a job here?

"Now that you know of the lines, let me present you with a dilemma The Council and I—as a realtor—are facing. Two witches have petitioned to buy a house that is on the market. The home sits here." She points to a small outcropping on the middle branch. I can't tell of it is in wing or fin territory, but it's definitely not witch. "They want to turn the house into a sort of library. A central hub for mythical knowledge, where all are allowed to learn."

The idea sounds glorious to me. "Are you going to let them? That's a place I'd like to visit."

Moira reclines against the couch, folding her hands over her stomach with a thoughtful tilt to her brows. "I imagine it would be popular. At least for those who are for sharing knowledge."

If only that were everyone.

"I would think the selkies would want access to all the knowledge they could get," I murmur, my mind flitting back to Seamus's library.

"Why's that?" Moira's voice is almost too casual.

Still half–caught up in the memory of the first time I visited her brother's library, I don't consider if I should keep my mouth shut.

"With more knowledge, the closer you will be to figuring out who or what that creepy creature was that tried to steal a selkie skin."

The realtor stiffens, and I blink away the mental image of that terrifying sketch.

"How do you know about that?" Her question lands between us, placed carefully with tension-strung words.

"Seamus. I saw the sketch," I explain, hoping I haven't gotten him in trouble, and then I wonder when exactly my mind-set about the man shifted from wanting to skewer him to wanting to protect him. "He said he couldn't find anything in his research. But maybe the witches would have something in the library they want to build."

Moira watches me for a moment, gaze assessing. When she next speaks, I think I might have scored well on whatever internal rubric she is comparing me to.

"That is a good point," she concedes. "But the property is in Of the Wing territory. If witches can buy property there, then why not grant every cross-boundary request?"

"Uh …" I try to figure out how to phrase my question without sounding like an ass. "I guess I'm wondering that too. What purpose exactly do the borders serve?"

Moira's expression is half-grimace, half-smile. "That's the same thing one of the witches asked. I believe the initial boundaries were meant as a sort of reparations. It wasn't about dividing mythics, but granting land to those who had suffered at the hands of The Collector. Dividing his massive property among the people he'd hurt. Those who wanted to stay in this area anyway. As to why the lines between our kinds still exist today? My best answer is, security. Every mythic exists with a certain level of fear. An understanding that if the wider world discovers our truth, we might lose everything we cherish. But here, there is not only a town for mythics, but also specific plots of land set aside for them beside others of their kind. As a realtor, you would also partly be a steward of Folk Haven. Working to maintain that sense of security."

A noise comes out of the back of my throat, agreement tinged with uncertainty. "I guess the way I grew up—suppressing every aspect of my mythic side—means I don't have a strong sense of myself as a siren." My mind traces over my childhood, and the landscape comes off as bleak and lonely. "I would have loved to live near any mythic. Not just someone Of the Wing. That's probably why the divides don't seem important to me. At least, not the ones between mythics. It's not each other we have to fear, right?"

Unconsciously, my eyes trace a path up the leftmost branch to the area Moira denoted as belonging to the monsters. The creatures born from mythics that are not of the same kind. Silently, I acknowledge that not all mythics share my views.

If I were to mate with someone like Seamus and have his child, then they'd be labeled a monster. Told to live in that one space designated to them. Maybe that section of Lake Galen is gorgeous, but my entire body rejects the notion of a judgment like that placed on someone because of their birth. A fact they have no control over.

"I'm not sure real estate is for me." There's more I could say on the subject, but as much as these strange designations discomfort me, I don't blame Moira for their existence. But I also don't want to take part in maintaining the divide.

She nods, but only half her attention seems to be on me while another part of her mind focuses elsewhere. "I understand. And you've given me another perspective to think about." The selkie blinks and draws all of her focus back to the room and to me. "Thank you for considering my offer. And keep in mind that The Council also represents you as long as you live in Folk Haven. If you have petitions or concerns, you can always bring them to your representative, Georgiana Stormwind. A siren. Sonya would have her contact information."

"Thank you. That's good to know." As I rise from the couch, I sweep my gaze over the map again, identifying the spot where Seamus's house sits. Perfectly situated in Of the Fin territory. If things went on a different path and we mated, would I be allowed to live in his magnificent home with its dream of a library? Or would we need to leave and build a new home?

I guess life is easier now that I never have to bother with those questions.

19

SEAMUS

SOMETHING about the predawn glow draws me to the shore. A knowledge lingering in the recesses of my mind—that as the darkness of the night recedes, so does my safety.

Other sleek bodies glide beside mine, skimming through the murky water with ease. When the lakebed rises in front of me, the ground a mixture of clay and stones, I know to press my front limbs into a special spot on my chest. A seam appears, and in a smooth motion, I divest myself of the connection to my other half.

My selkie skin.

"There you are, my boy. How are you feeling? Good swim?" The gruff voice comes with a strong arm around my waist.

I sway into the warm hold as the cool morning air traces over my exposed body.

"Dad." I grin at the man, saying nothing more. Why talk when there's nothing to say that could make this good feeling any better?

I am refreshed. Rejuvenated. Invigorated.

And slightly clumsy on my feet.

"Lean on me. I'll get you up the hill. Don't want to plant your face in the ground and eat dirt, do you? Not when I've got such a nice breakfast prepared."

"Waffles," I agree.

My head lolls on my shoulders, heavy with fluffy cotton. As my chin tilts to the side, I notice more family trekking not too far off. Owen and Calder stumble along just to the left of us with Delta between them.

"She's stronger than you," I slur to my father, which earns me a deep chuckle in response. I like the way his joyful noise tickles my ears.

"Well, she's a dragon. And I'm a mere mortal, who already carried his wife up this hill ten minutes ago. Give an old man some slack." My dad pulls open the door that leads into the large sitting room of their home.

"My skin!" I yelp, suddenly remembering the importance of that priceless piece of me through the fog of happiness.

"Got it right here." Dad holds up his other arm, so I can see the shimmering pelt he carries.

Relief washes through me, and he grunts as I relax so much that my knees bend.

"Couch. Now. You're going to throw my back out, son."

"Get a golf cart," I offer, collapsing across the cushions on one half of the sectional. "Be a chauffeur."

"Just might," he grumbles while spreading my selkie hide over my body. "You lie there and sober up."

"Not drunk," I protest without any conviction.

"We have this same argument every month. I'm going to record my answers and start playing them for you, so I don't need to waste my breath."

"Orange juice," I say instead of trying to come up with a response.

He snorts and strolls away. A moment later, I have a tall

glass of vitamin C and a plate full of food in my lap. In addition to waffles, there are home fries and sausage links and a pile of scrambled eggs. Only takes me minutes to shovel the delicious mass down.

No one makes breakfast better than Malcolm MacNamara.

"Malcolm MacNamara," I mutter aloud, chuckling at the alliteration.

Dad took Mama's last name when they mated, as is selkie custom.

"Calder Novac," I say, not as impressed with my brother's mash-up.

"Seamus Onassis," I sigh to myself, tasting the delicious pairing on my lips.

With a full stomach and happy buzz, I relax back on the couch, my head resting on the cushy armrest. My spot gives me a clear view of the entire room, which holds multiple selkies recovering from a long night's swim. Owen lies facedown on the floor, snoring loud enough to wake the neighbors. His best friend, Finn, lounges in an overstuffed recliner across the way. The man is human, but he cradles our family friend Isla, his selkie mate, in his lap, holding her glass of orange juice while she eats at a more sedate pace than I did. On the other half of the sectional, Delta sits upright, and Calder uses her thighs as a pillow, smiling in bliss as she carefully combs her little claws through his curly hair.

My own blissful state flags as a cloud of jealousy drifts into my happy place.

Where's my cuddle buddy? Where's my loving mate who I can wrap my body around and pet and stroke and feed food to and be fed by?

This is some bullshit.

When I try to imagine a partner next to me, one face appears in my mind over and over again.

Neri.

What I wouldn't give to have her fresh-rain scent surrounding me. Her fingers, rough from that hot espresso machine, tracing over my sensitive skin. Her plump lips pressing sweet kisses on my face before parting to whisper naughty thoughts in my ear.

I want my Neri.

I have enough presence of mind to set my cup and plate on the side table before heaving myself up from the couch, keeping my pelt wrapped around me, more because the skin feels good on mine than because I'm butt-ass naked underneath.

Selkies have little modesty after a dark moon swim.

With steps only slightly steadier than when I rose from the lake, I navigate to the guest bedroom and find my pile of belongings, including my phone. I collapse on the mattress, taking multiple tries to swipe to the screen I want.

My attempts at flirting in the café were too subtle. I need to take a more direct approach. But I also need to be suave. Confident. Charming.

I've never felt surer of myself in my life.

With a cocky grin, I type out a text to Neri. Hit Send.

Then, I type another.

And another.

And another ...

20

———

NERI

AFTER MY INFORMATIVE meeting with Moira MacNamara yesterday, I have trouble sleeping. But not because anything she said
caused mental anguish. Yeah, there are aspects of the political
and social structure of Folk Haven I'm not a fan of, but none of
them currently affect me.

What keeps me up at night is the failure to find my calling.

Moira's crisp business card in my wallet gave me hope that
there was a new career on the horizon.

Now that the promise is gone and I'm back to agonizing
over what I'm going to do with my life, I need to come up with a
plan.

First thing on the agenda: smash my phone.

I was struggling to fall asleep before, and the regular
buzzing for the last twenty minutes has made the task
impossible.

"Fine," I groan after what must be the dozenth vibration.
Pushing aside my covers, I sit up and flick on my bedside lamp.
If the buzzing had come at the regular intervals, indicating a

call, I would've gotten up sooner. Calls at early hours likely mean emergencies.

But who texts at six a.m.?

Wiping the bleariness from my eyes, I unplug my phone from the charger and stare down at the screen.

Sixteen new messages.

All from Seamus MacNamara.

"What the hell?" With zero grace, I plop down on my pillows and swipe to open my texts.

Seamus: Your hair is quite good.

If I thought reading the messages would clarify things, they sure as hell don't. Each one gets more nonsensical. Is butt-texting a thing? Because I think Seamus might have sent me his entire ass in the form of random words.

Seamus: When you hug. Hows that?

Seamus: Bet your strong like dragon.

Seamus: Your eyes are not purple.

Seamus: There silver.

Seamus: Ive looked at them deeply.

Seamus: With my eyes.

Seamus: Hows cuddling?

Seamus: Would you?

Seamus: I'll give you books. All of them.

Well, that last one is tempting even though I still have no clue what I'm reading.

Since sleep has officially eluded me, I carry my phone into the bathroom, rereading the string of texts as I brush my teeth.

Could he be in trouble? Is this some strange code to let me know he's been kidnapped?

With that thought, I figure there's no harm in calling him. Just to check.

But the phone goes straight to voice mail.

Did he ignore my call, or is something going on?

Anxiety slowly creeps through my chest as I press to call again.

Voice mail again. This time, I leave a message.

"Hey, Seamus. I just got a bunch of random texts from you. Were they supposed to make sense? Are you okay?" I pause and then make a decision. "I'm coming over to check on you. Because you're freaking me out. If this is all a misunderstanding, call me, and I'll turn my ass around. See you in a bit."

I end the call and quickly change my clothes, opting for comfort over cuteness. Not sure what the rest of my morning will turn into, I grab a Pop-Tart on my way out the front door. No reason to be confused *and* hungry.

A short while later, I turn onto the road that stretches down the inlet, where a good chunk of selkies live. Just as I follow a curve around a collection of trees and spy the end of Seamus's driveway up ahead, I also spot a figure meandering along the side of the road, coming toward me from the opposite direction.

A little closer, and I realize I've found Seamus.

And he doesn't look exactly firm on his feet.

"Hey!" I call out my open window and then hurriedly pull my car off the side of the road, pressing down the parking brake before shutting things off and hopping out.

"Neri!" The way the selkie says my name, with that wide grin and glowing eyes, has my feet stumbling, but I keep moving forward until we're right in front of each other.

"What's up? I woke up to a bunch of strange texts from you, and then you wouldn't pick up when I called." And as I stare into his eyes, I watch as they go in and out of focus.

"They weren't strange." He sounds put out, the full-grown man pouting down at me. "They were *suave*."

"Okay, sure." Even though I have zero clue what's going on, I realize Seamus is not in the proper state to debate the nuances of language. "Are you drunk? You seem unsteady."

"Mmm." The satisfied noise he makes comes from deep in

his chest and sends all those fluttery, looping, soaring sensations tumbling through my body again.

Then, Seamus MacNamara, esteemed professor, boops my nose.

The gesture throws me off so much that I can only gape up at him.

"So cute. I want to cuddle."

The nose boop surprised me, but the experience of the selkie wrapping a set of sturdy yet gentle arms around my body has my whole world rearranging.

Because I like it.

So, *so* much.

And I find myself twining my own arms around his waist, pressing myself into his cotton T-shirt, stretched over his warm chest. And praise The Winged One, the mixture of soft and hard is enough to melt a woman's brain.

This is a different version of Seamus than I've ever encountered before—and not just because of the slight slur in his voice. The normally buttoned-up professor is dressed down. He's sporting a threadbare T-shirt with Ramla's logo printed across the chest and a pair of sweatpants that hang in exactly the right way off his hips. And he's got on sandals.

I can see his toes.

When did toes become something hot? It's not like I want to suck on them or anything.

Why am I thinking about sucking on toes?

The odd train of thought runs straight off the tracks, and I need to get back in line. But focusing is wildly difficult when his distracting body presses all along mine. He smells like warm clay and soap, the scent so earthy and raw.

"Okay, buddy." I let one arm drop away, so I can turn us down the driveway, keeping my other arm hooked around his waist. "Why don't we get you inside?"

"Fine," he sighs, as if I asked him to drive me to the Atlanta

Airport during rush hour. But he moves his ass forward at a slow, swaying pace.

"Where were you walking home from?" I ask because the idea of him in this loopy state, meandering along the side of the road, terrifies me. But once the words are out of my mouth, all I can think of is him spending a drunken night with some woman.

Am I assisting a man who is only just sobering up after a night of wild escapades?

No need to home in on why that makes me so livid. This is what *friends* do.

"My parents'."

The maelstrom in my chest eases.

Seamus fumbles a key out of his pocket, and after a couple of tries, he is able to slide it home.

"Did you all have five a.m. mimosas or something?"

Are the MacNamaras party animals?

His head shake is slow, and all the while, he shines a goofy smile down at me. "Went for a swim."

"A swim?" My skin goose bumps at the thought of submerging my body in Lake Galen without the sun shining to make my skin toasty first. "This early in the morning?"

Seamus keeps his hold on me as he shuffles toward the library. I should probably leave him be.

But what if he's sick, and that's why he's so out of it?

"Swam all night," the selkie declares before finally releasing me. He collapses onto one of the cushier couches and smiles up at me.

That's when the date registers in my mind. Last night was a dark moon. Sonya mentioned that's when selkies wear their other skins and swim in Lake Galen. The darkness hides the mythics from anyone who might be on the lake after sunset. My cousin told me it was a good night for sirens to take to the sky. If I wanted to stretch my wings.

But I haven't.

I just can't. Not yet.

"Cuddle with me." Seamus stretches out fully on the piece of furniture and then raises his arms in invitation.

And what a lovely offer it is. But I shake my head.

"If I lie down with you, I'll fall asleep." Or I'll lie there in a state of perpetual, unfulfilled arousal, which can't be fun for anyone involved.

"So, fall asleep. I'm going to. Haven't slept all night." He wiggles his shoulders, sinking further into the pillows.

Gods, he looks comfy. And not just the state he's in, but also the man himself. I want to drape my body over his body and soak up his relaxation.

Maybe I could cuddle. Just for a little bit.

"Okay." I toe off my shoes and then sit on the edge of a cushion, trying to figure out the best arrangement.

Seamus hooks his arms around me and pulls my back flush with his chest.

"We're spooning?" I get the words out the moment before a yawn cracks through my jaw.

The selkie murmurs something about eating me with a spoon, but sleep already has her delicious claws in me, and I sink into unconsciousness before I can decide how I feel about his suggestive words.

21

———

SEAMUS

MY DREAMS HAVE CRAFTED themselves into reality. Everything about this feels real, but holding Neri against my chest as we lie on my favorite couch in my favorite room is a fantasy.

A fantasy that involves her drooling on my arm.

That's not a detail I expected my brain to add, but when the synapses are firing off to give me something as amazing as this, who cares what odd little quirks get added in? Like the tickle of her hair under my chin and the chafe of my sweatpants against my hard dick.

That's all fine when I get to pretend this is real life and enjoy the way my memory has drawn up the exact scent of her fresh-rain smell.

Even earning a PhD never had me wanting to shake my brain's hand so much as in this moment.

"Ung," dream Neri grunts as she shifts against me.

Her butt presses backward into my greedy erection that suddenly seems too solid for dreamland.

But that would mean—

"Seamus?"

This is real.

"Yeah?" The word rasps from my throat, and I clear the sleepy disbelief from my voice as best I can.

"You're awake." This time, when Neri shifts, it's not backward but around. She turns her body in my arms until we're face-to-face.

She has to know I'm hard. There's no way to hide the length between us unless I shove a wooden board in front of my dick to keep everything flat. Still, she doesn't make any move or indication she notices.

"How are you feeling?"

"Me? Great!" *That was enthusiastic.* "Fine, I mean. Good. Swell." *Finned One, please take my ability to speak.*

But Neri's slow-blooming smile truly has the power to render me speechless. "Well, you're still not your normal self, but you don't sound drunk anymore."

And that's when my memories flood in. The dark moon swim. The envy at seeing my brother with his mate. Stumbling around for my phone.

The texts.

"Fuck," I groan, turning my face so I can smash it into a throw pillow and hide from reality.

"Hey there." A firm pressure against my neck feels an awful lot like her hand on my bare skin, and every ounce of my will goes to making sure my hips don't rock forward with the pleasure of the touch. "Can you look at me? Tell me what happened this morning? You were really out of it, and I still don't know why."

Of course she doesn't. Dragging in a breath and shoving down my mortification to deal with later, I rotate my head until I meet her silvery stare. So close. Just a few inches between our faces. I could kiss her. Just lean in and press my mouth against her plush lips.

But I've been enough of an ass for the day. For the decade really.

"When a selkie hasn't worn their skin for a stretch and then they go on a long swim, the experience can be intoxicating. The sunrise seems to be what sets us off. That's what happened. I was as good as wasted this morning. Damn The Finned One's games." I shut my eyes, taking another moment to push away the mortification. "I remember texting you, but I have no idea what I said. Please tell me there wasn't anything offensive."

Neri studies me and then shrugs with a secret little smile flicking at the corner of those lips I want to kiss. "Not offensive. Complimentary, if anything. You said I have good hair."

My gaze immediately tracks to her mussed yet still-silky white-blonde locks. "You do."

A rosy tinge rises in her cheeks, and I watch the color shift with fascination.

"You said I was as strong as a dragon."

"Of course I did," I grumble to myself. But I take comfort in the fact that Neri is here in my arms and that she seems to mainly take amusement from the experience. "What else?"

"You talked about my eyes."

"That's no surprise when I'm often lost in them."

That earns me a tiny gasp. I can't stop staring into those metallic irises now as silence stretches between us. I'm at a loss for why I ever pushed Neri away. Why I ever entertained the notion that she's something other than the perfect partner.

"You said you'd give me all your books," she whispers.

Even as I attempt a fearsome scowl, a grin breaks through. "You're taking advantage."

"Nope." Her lips pop on the *P*, and the sound ricochets through my torso, bouncing off every vital organ. "I have it in writing. No take-backs."

There's a pull deep in my body, tugging me toward her, even though we're almost as close as two people can be. But every word Neri speaks has me wanting to sink into this connection between us and never leave. That won't keep her from walking away though.

"To be clear, you aren't upset with me?"

"Of course not." Neri reaches up to smooth her fingers over my wrinkled brow. "If anything, I'm envious. You think waiting a month to take on your other form is a long time? Try twenty-five years."

Shock stiffens my previously liquid limbs. "What?"

My enchanting siren nods, allowing her neck to relax until her head rests on my arm. "I haven't spread my wings since I was five years old."

"Gods, Neri. That must be …" There's no way I can think of the proper word to end the sentence.

I try to imagine what life would be like if I hadn't taken my selkie form for multiple decades. But I can't manage it. The concept is unfathomable. My body would wither and die.

"I'm used to it," she says with a shrug. "I can barely remember"—her voice catches on that single word, betraying her true desolation under her casual tone—"what they feel like."

"Why have you gone so long?"

"My parents. My mother mainly. She's a siren; my father is a human, but he knows. She decided that because sirens don't have to sing or unfurl our wings, we shouldn't. Living life as humans was safer. So, she taught me to keep everything inside. Buttoned up." The silver in Neri's eyes glints as she offers me a small smile. "The times I sang at you were acts of rebellion, you might say."

"You should rebel more often." I press a kiss to her forehead because the smooth skin is just near my mouth, and from the raw nerves in her voice, I get the sense that Neri could use some comforting.

"It does feel good. To use my voice like I haven't before."

"Do you want to stretch your wings?"

Instead of giving a direct answer, Neri smooths a flat palm over my chest, just above my heart. "They're large. Very obvious. Not easy to hide, I mean. There aren't a lot of places I can open them without the risk of people spotting me." Her teeth dig into her bottom lip and then let the soft skin slide free. "And I missed the night of the dark moon."

The longing and devastation in her voice tell me all that I need to know.

Neri wants to embrace this part of herself desperately.

And I'll do anything I can to help her.

"No need for darkness. And the library is plenty big enough." Gently, I stroke a hand over her shoulder blades, knowing just beneath the fabric of her shirt, there are two lines in her flesh that mark the place her wings hide away. "Why don't you open them in here?"

22

NERI

"*Open them in here.*"

I don't know how long I let those words spread through my body, as if they had soaring wings themselves. But next time I come back to myself, I realize I'm standing, leaving Seamus in his prone position on the couch.

He stays there, sprawled out, looking how I imagined The Finned One might appear on their dais of coral if they assumed the shape of a man. If the selkie had continued to speak, to push, I would have shoved back. Argued with all the words my mother had put in my head and my mouth over the years.

I don't need to open my wings.

If I do open them, they might come out again at an inopportune moment.

Letting them go is dangerous.

Wanting to fly is selfish.

But Seamus lets me work through the silent arguments on my own. He simply waits, his liquid brown eyes following my pacing around the library. So much room here with the ceiling soaring high above us and the length of the space extravagant in its vastness.

You're not going to fly anywhere. No exposure.

Just stretching underused limbs.

Exploring pieces of myself I haven't seen since my childhood.

"What if they're gone?" I whisper, my voice hoarse with fear. *Can that happen? Would the gods have taken back my gift, thinking I didn't deserve the beautiful part of myself because I'd hidden them away, as if I were ashamed?*

Seamus sits up and slides to the edge of the couch, clutching his hands between his knees. "I don't like drawing conclusions before a study has even gotten underway."

His academic speak somehow soothes me, easing away a touch of my fear. My gaze tracks over him with his submissive posture.

If I try this, I will reveal a personal part of myself. My true form, siren wings on display. Or I will show Seamus how I appear in the depths of despair if I find my wings have abandoned me.

To be fair, the man was just vulnerable with me. Calling me to him when he was defenseless after a dark moon swim. If I'd wanted to hurt him, that would have been an easy time to do so.

I'm safe here. And I need to know.

"Okay. I'll do it."

Seamus nods, keeping his same position on the couch. This is all on me. Every step is my choice. My freedom is something I have to grasp myself. Suddenly, my clothes weigh heavy on my body. I tug off the T-shirt over my head and toss it to the side. Next is my bra, baring my back to the room.

An image pops into my mind of a style of shirt I've seen multiple sirens wear. There's only a thin strip of fabric tracing down the spine, but otherwise, the shoulders and lower back are fully exposed.

That way, they can draw their wings out at any time. If this goes well, I'll need to get some of those shirts.

Then, I notice Seamus's stare dragging over my naked chest.

Maybe I don't need one of them.

I shake my head and refocus on my task. This isn't the first pair of tits the man has seen. He'll get over it.

"Okay," I say more to myself than to him. "Let's do this."

Despite lack of use, the muscles that control my wings are familiar. I tense them, pushing at the slight barrier—a shield of magic that naturally formed with my body. With hope and trepidation, I coax the limbs free.

There's a pressure, a snap, and then ...

Relief.

More than that. There's ecstasy.

"Oh!" I gasp, leaning forward to brace my hands on my knees as I deal with the pleasure rolling through me. No cramps. No pins and needles. No flare of agony.

If anything, my body has gone lighter. As if I'm about to float off the ground.

With these good feelings coursing through my veins, I easily push aside my anxiety to glance over my shoulder and see what's become of my old friends.

They've grown with me.

Large dove-gray wings sprout from my shoulders. The tips almost brush the floor, and I know instinctively that my wings' expanse will sprawl wider than I am tall if I extend them. Reaching behind myself, I stroke my fingers over the soft yet sturdy feathers. Not many would guess this beauty has lived inside my body all these years. Tucked away in some magical pocket that shrank them down to travel size.

But now, I can stretch. I roll my shoulders, my neck, easing into the relief. How much weight have I been carrying inside me?

"Hello," I whisper to the pieces of me I feared I would never get a chance to greet again. "Long time."

With an excited grin, I face forward, expecting Seamus to have a curious look on his face. Maybe a question ready to be posed, like the academic he is.

But the selkie does not look like he is in the middle of garnering knowledge.

The man stares at me as if I'm The Winged One come to browse his humble library.

"Seamus?"

"By the gods. You're magnificent," he groans out the compliment, and my nipples tighten in response. Which he has a front row seat to since I am currently topless.

Not knowing how to answer or if I want to, instead, I spread my wings wide, stretching them to their full capacity, close to tears that I have the room and freedom to do so. Each subtle shift sends more pleasure shooting through my nerve endings. This form does not take precedence over my wingless one but exists as an equal part. A side that has been underfed. Underserved.

For now—even if the moment is brief—I want to live in this shape. Let my siren nature breathe. Experience life as the mythic I am and always have been.

My eyes track back to Seamus, finding the selkie biting hard into his lip, hands fisted at his sides, as if he has to force himself to keep from touching me.

And that's when I realize just how much I need his hands on me.

This body deserves to be worshipped.

23

───────

SEAMUS

THIS IS what humans must have felt like when the gods first appeared before them.

Awe.

Neri takes measured steps toward me, not drowning in the same desperate wave I am. She is a powerful beauty with her body proudly displayed, magnificent wings sprawling from her back. The feathers shimmer, as if made of metal. Their color matches her eyes, a silver so sharp that it easily pierces straight to my heart.

"I haven't existed in this state in decades," her lyrical voice reminds me.

Neri pauses, just out of reach. Not that I'm trying to grab her.

My body demands that I do exactly that. But I keep to my seat.

"You are welcome here anytime," I rasp. "Day or night. You should open your wings whenever you wish."

"Night, huh?"

The teasing note in her voice drags my gaze up from her puckered nipples.

When I meet her eyes, my breath catches.

Could that be lust? Could she feel something akin to the draw I have toward her?

"I always want you here," I confess. It's the truth.

Now that she's spent time in my house, the place echoes empty without the delicate sound of her flipping a page. I need her fresh-rain scent to linger on every surface. If I had any skill with a camera, I'd ask to take her photo, so I could hang images of her in every room.

That way, I could delude myself into believing this was where I'd always find her.

"Do you want to touch me?"

The question hits me harder than a bear shifter's punch to the gut, shoving out a bark of laughter that sounds much like the seal I resemble in my other form. "I'm considering breaking the bones in my hands to keep them from clutching at you without your permission. Yes, Neri. I ache to touch you."

The siren takes one final step, placing herself in the space between my legs.

"This body deserves to be admired. I've hidden myself away for too long." With curious fingers, she combs through my wildly curling hair. "Touch me, please. I need it."

And I need nothing more than that permission. My hands fly forward, slowing only an inch from her skin so that I can spread my fingers wide and press my entire palm to her bare belly. Neri sucks in a breath at the contact and then leans into the pressure.

"Bless The Finned One," I mutter as my hands ease across her smooth skin, circling her waist, drawing up in an erotic glide that brings my thumbs to the undersides of her breasts.

"Mmm," Neri hums deep in her throat as her touch rests on

the back of my neck. Not directing me anywhere, but claiming me all the same.

I heft the weight of her breasts and then stroke across her nipples, slowly caressing the peaks jutting toward me.

"Can I taste you?" My question spills from my chest before I can debate if asking for too much will mean I lose everything.

"Only if your hands keep touching," Neri murmurs.

Raising my scrutiny from her body, I find the siren has her eyes closed. Beautiful gaze shielded from me.

Not right, I think. *I need to see her soul through her eyes.*

Following her command, I map the curve of her spine with my hands as I rest her stiff peak on my lower lip, all the while keeping my eyes up, ready for hers whenever she gives them back to me. With a quick flick, I snake my tongue out, tasting her.

Neri's body jerks, her nails digging into the base of my skull with a delicious sting. But the best moment is when her lids flutter open, stare adhering to mine. That's when I suck her nipple into my mouth, plying the sensitive spot with hot breaths and needy nips of my teeth.

"Seamus." The way she says my name, on a gasp of surprise, as if she never expected this from me, clicks something into place in my brain. In my heart.

The gods were right.

Maybe the lore of selkie mates is just a story we pass down that some of our kind take too literally. But in this moment, I know it applies to me perfectly.

Neri saved my life.

Completely unrelated to that, Neri is the woman I want at my side always. I want to hear my name on her lips in that exact tone every day for the rest of my existence.

The light around us dims, and the shift surprises me into letting her slide from my mouth. Then, I realize the reason behind the darkness.

Neri's wings encircle me, sheltering the two of us in a cocoon of feathers and majesty.

"Can I touch them?" This close, I can study the fiber of every feather, but I want to know the sensation of them against my fingers.

"Please do." Muscles tense under the skin in her shoulders, and her wings draw closer until I experience a light brush at my back.

I've kept my hands just below her shoulder blades, but now, I guide them upward until I meet that fascinating place where skin morphs into feather.

Neri groans, but there's no pain in the exhale. Only relief, as if I'm massaging a deep ache in a tight muscle for her.

"More," she demands.

I'm happy to comply.

Despite their color and shimmer, her wings are not formed from metal. Instead, the texture reminds me of smooth silk, almost liquid against my palms. Keeping my hands flat, I trail along the length where they surround me, watching the quiver that follows my path. When I have to turn to explore further, I retrace my journey, watching the play of silver through my fingers.

By the time I return to skin, we're both panting.

Neri releases my neck, and I'm suddenly terrified she's going to step away.

Instead, the siren slips her thumbs into her waistband, and with a shimmy of her hips, she pushes off the sweatpants that hid the rest of her body from my hungry gaze.

"More," she repeats. This time, there's no demand. Just hope.

Neri doesn't know yet that I'll spend the rest of my life fulfilling all her hopes. Best I start now.

I palm her ass, a smile curling my lips as the taut globes clench when I dig my fingers into them. With a firm grip, I urge her closer, scooting to the edge of my seat. When Neri's curls are just in front of my face and her rain scent mixes with the tang of arousal, I send a silent thank-you to the gods. And an apology for ever doubting them.

Then, I press a kiss to both sides of her hips as my hands draw to the front, thumbs stroking against her pussy lips before parting them to reveal her slick vulva.

"Can I touch you here?" I ask, knowing my words must vibrate against her private skin.

"Yes. I want you there." She cups the back of my head, urging me forward. As if I need any more encouragement.

At the first swipe of my tongue, I am in nirvana, and my siren has to grip my shoulders for support. The shelter of her wings disappears but only because her long-hidden limbs flutter with each pass of my tongue. As if her clit has a direct line to her wings.

"Don't stop," she sobs out, rocking against my mouth.

Never, I promise silently.

When Neri comes, I taste the victory on my tongue and hear the cry of ecstasy all the way to my bones. Worried her knees might give out, I grasp her waist in a tight hold, lending her my strength.

For a time, the only sounds in the library are the rushing pants from my siren in recovery from her orgasm.

A strong grip wraps around my wrists. When I meet Neri's eyes, her silver burns molten. She tears my hands from her body, and I groan in despair at the loss of her.

Please don't run from me. I don't deserve you, but, gods, I want you.

Just as I'm about to start bargaining, willing to give her anything for a chance to prove myself worthy, I realize my siren isn't retreating. She hasn't even let me go.

Instead, Neri pushes me backward, looming over me.

"Do you have any condoms in this library?"

The practical question takes too long to pierce through the lust coating my brain.

"Seamus!" She tightens her hold on my wrists, maybe as desperate as I am.

"Desk!" I gasp the word, thanking The Finned One I listened to my dick last time I was at the drugstore.

Was it a fantasy or premonition that played through my mind in the store? A scene of Neri bending over my desk, legs splayed, back arched as I slid past her wet pussy lips.

She retreats, and with a flick of her wings, she half-leaps, half-glides to the piece of furniture, pulling out drawers until she comes up with the unopened box. In a blink, Neri returns to her dominate position over me.

"If you don't say stop, I'm going to mount you," she informs me in a harsh crack of her voice, the sharp edges honed to a point by need.

"Gods, yes. I need you. Use me. Take from me. Anything you want." The agreements spill out, all combinations of words just to get her to follow through on the promise in her smoldering gaze.

"Lie back."

Neri cups my hard length through my sweatpants. My hips jerk off the couch cushions, even as I try to stay prone.

She makes quick work of my clothes, pushing my shirt up my chest and over my head, and then she drags my pants down my legs. Sprawled out naked on the couch, I gaze at her as she looms above me.

Perfection.

Then, she slings a leg over my hips, her bare core on display, glistening from the orgasm I helped her achieve. The siren grips my dick, pausing for a moment to fondle my foreskin, drawing the flesh up over the sensitive head until I'm on the edge of ecstasy. With a tear of foil and confident movements, Neri sheaths me in the protection, rolling the rubber to my base.

"I'll do anything for you." The promise comes on a gasp as her palm lands flat on my chest, just over my heart.

NERI

Seamus's words are heavy, and yet I am light as air.

Maybe sirens are similar to selkies when it comes to our other halves because I'm currently getting drunk off this experience. His groans are intoxicating. The slide of our hot skin hypnotizing. The scent of aroused man mixed with old book pages is an ambrosia I expect the gods sip of daily.

"This is what I want." I demonstrate by holding him upright, pressing his engorged cock against the swollen folds of my vulva. My body jerks at the contact so soon after an orgasm, but a moment later, as I sink down onto him, everything is smooth and delicious. No shocks. Just sensual easing.

Seamus's fingers dig into my hips hard at my claiming. The academic has lost control of his senses, and I devour his gasping curses by diving in for a kiss just as I sit fully on him. He tastes as good as he looks, rich and fresh. Maybe Lake Galen purified his body for me. Presented me with the rawest form of this mythic man.

The selkie rocks his hips, massaging the inside of me, drawing more pleasure to my nerve endings than any partner has achieved before.

"Seamus," I moan his name, sitting tall so I can gaze down at him while I ride.

"Gods," he chokes out, and I can't stop the triumphant curve of my mouth as I watch a muscle strain taut in his neck at the relentless pace I set.

A glint in the corner of my eye pulls my attention away from the man between my thighs. I realize immediately the glimmer is nothing more than the midday sun reflecting off the water outside the library's windows.

The view through the glass is glorious. Mesmerizing. I can almost imagine myself gliding over the lake.

And the fantasy takes hold.

My wings, which were relaxed at my back as I focused on my pleasure, spread wide now. I extend them to their full length, as if I were suspended in the air, soaring across the mirror surface of the water, trees flashing by me on either side, complete freedom in every inch of my body.

As the image becomes solid in my mind, a firm pressure strokes my clit.

"Oh!" The exclamation bursts from my lips on a gust of exhilarated ecstasy.

As another orgasm takes hold of my body, my wings flex, my pussy contracts, and my eyes drop to meet a set of liquid brown that stare up at me. I'm too lost in the physical sensations of my body to read the emotions passing across Seamus's face.

The next instant, he's sitting up, one arm pressing me tight to his hips. There's a desperation in the gasping note of his breath. Even in my hazy mind, I know he hovers on the same edge I soared off a second ago.

I sigh, draping my arms over his shoulders and nuzzling my face into his neck. At the corner of his jaw, I kiss and suck the salty sweat from his skin, wondering if this is what the ocean tastes like.

"Let go," I breathe against his hammering pulse.

Seamus barks out a noise on the verge of pain, and then his cock jerks inside me, spilling his orgasm.

And for one glorious moment, I don't doubt that I am in the exact place I should be.

24

———

SEAMUS

A FEATHER TICKLES MY NOSE, and I blow it away with a quick puff of breath. The piece of Neri drifts through the air, floating leisurely over our satiated forms.

My siren lies, warm and pliant, on top of me. Her body fits perfectly against mine as we press close enough to feel each other's heavy heartbeats. I've never enjoyed this utter contentment before. Not after previous sexual encounters. Not after reading a favorite book or teaching a successful class. Not even after a night of swimming in my selkie form.

All those things pale in comparison to having Neri Onassis in my arms.

If I wasn't so relaxed, I'd berate myself for pushing her away in the first place. I almost lost this. Lost us.

A fearsome growl rumbles between our bodies. The sound makes me smile.

"That's your fault." Neri lifts her head off my chest to hit me with a teasing glare. "All I had for breakfast was a Pop-Tart because I rushed out the door to see if you'd knocked your head against something."

When I chuckle, she bounces from my spasming diaphragm, which only makes me laugh more. Then, the gorgeous woman sits upright, and I groan, almost pained by the sight of her. But when I reach out to fondle her delicious curves, the haughty siren slaps my hands away and dismounts from my hips. Every part of me misses her, a chill biting over the previously hot places where we were pressed together.

"You're responsible for feeding me," Neri announces as she scoops up her pants.

"Fine. I guess you deserve a treat after all the hard work you did." Memories of her riding me threaten to harden my cock again. I ease the condom off and tie the neck before tossing it in a small bin next to the couch.

Neri smirks over her shoulder as she bends to grab her shirt and bra. "You'd better believe I do. Maybe you can manage something without burning down your kitchen this time."

I fake a snarl and launch off the couch after her, swiping my arms around her waist. Neri giggles as I lift her off the ground, and her wings flutter as I spin her around. This position puts her sweet nipples at the exact right height for my mouth. I can't stop myself from sucking the tempting tip just past my lips.

"Seamus!" Neri gasps out my name as she wraps her arms around my head and legs around my waist, dropping her gathered clothes to the floor with a muffled thump. My siren rocks her hips against me with each tug of my mouth.

As her slick core presses against my feverish skin, my dick rises to the occasion once more. The rapid recovery, after I thought she'd rung every last drop of pleasure from me, spurs a desperation to be back inside her.

Mine, the word echoes through my brain, and I groan in agreement.

With stumbling steps, I get us to my desk, my hand scrambling for another condom the instant her ass lands on the wood. A second later, I'm pumping into her.

Neri's gasps turn into begging moans, her nails dragging across my back as she urges me on. When I need to feel her body fully accept mine, revel in those telltale clenches of her inner muscles, I reach a hand between us and thumb her clit.

The siren's wings spread wide, and she throws her head back, shouting out incoherent words as she bears down on my cock over and over, milking out another release that causes my vision to blur. I would fall to the floor if I didn't lock my knees.

As I come out of the orgasm haze, both of us breathe like we just ran a marathon in a matter of minutes. My body aches but in all of the best ways.

"You"—Neri sets her palms against my still-heaving chest —"are the definition of a hot professor."

I bury my face in her neck as I snort out laughter. "Good thing you didn't enroll." I press my lips to her salty skin. "Or else this would be a fireable offense."

"Well, I—" Another rolling rumble from her belly cuts Neri off. She punches me in the pec but not hard. "You distracted me again. Food. I need food."

As much as I don't want to separate my body from hers, what kind of mate would I be if I let my woman go hungry?

The word I just thought registers the moment I step out of her embrace.

Mate.

I just thought of Neri as my mate.

And ... I'm not panicking. If anything, a sense of calm settles deep in the core of my being.

Neri is my mate.

"Cereal is not going to cut it. I want something cooked. Preferably greasy." The siren keeps talking as she pulls on her pants, unaware of the new perspective I have.

Or maybe she is. I can't be the only one whose world shook

into a different alignment after what happened in the past hour.

Neri fiddles with her bra, and then after she wistfully glances over her shoulder, the glorious wings start to fold in on themselves, tucking every feather back into her skin until she stands before me, easily able to pass as a human. Then, regrettably, my siren dresses completely. I follow suit, getting rid of the second condom and tugging on my sweats as my mind shuffles through information.

One immediate conclusion arises. My mate needs to eat, and there's a whole buffet just down the road.

"Let's walk to my parents' house."

Neri pauses in the act of slipping on her shoes. "Why would we do that?"

"My dad makes a huge breakfast for the morning after a dark moon swim. There's still plenty set up." Excitement rises through me until I'm jittery with the urge to tow Neri toward my childhood home. "And everyone is there, so I can introduce you. I know you've met Moira and my brothers, but I'll introduce you to my mom and dad and some other selkies." I can't wait for everyone to get to know Neri past what they've seen of her behind the counter at the coffee shop.

My mate.

Neri doesn't respond right away, slowly sliding her shoes onto her feet.

"You want me to meet your family?" Neri's brows scrunch over her eyes when she finally glances up at me. "Why?"

The question has my brain tripping over itself. "Because we're ... I mean, we ... what we just did ... that was special." *Special?* More like world-altering. At least, I thought so. "Wasn't it?"

Neri crosses her arms over her chest. "We had great sex. Why does that mean I need to meet your family?"

"You don't *need* to." I press my fingers into my scalp, trying to dig out the right words to say. To clarify what I want us to be. "You can meet them later. After we go out more."

Neri's silver eyes spark at that. "Go out? You sound like you want to date me."

"Of course I do."

Her beautiful lips part in an O that I might find suggestive if a trickle of panic wasn't working through my chest. She snaps her mouth shut. "A few weeks ago, you acted like a relationship with me was the bubonic plague." All the lighthearted banter from earlier evaporates from Neri's eyes as she stares me down.

Frustration has me longing to pull my hair out by the roots, but I suck in a calming breath and take another go at the situation.

"That was an overreaction. I'm sorry. You know why I don't like the idea of something being *fated*. But I think the gods had it right. Look how well we get along." I gesture around the library that we both love and have now fucked in multiple times. "We seem to fit together."

If I thought Neri was stiff before, it's nothing compared to how she freezes now.

"Fit together?" She grits the words through clenched teeth. "So, this is suddenly easy? The idea of us dating?"

"Yes." Easy because this is *right*. I didn't see that before, but I do now.

The siren shakes her head, glaring past me instead of meeting my eyes.

"You know who I *seemed* to fit with?" she spits out. "Ronald Lancaster."

The name is unfamiliar to me, but the idea of Neri connecting herself to another man has a toxic pit opening up in my stomach. "What are you saying?"

"I'm saying that Ronald Lancaster fit me perfectly on paper. We met in college, both in the same business program. We started dating. His parents almost immediately became good friends with mine. When we graduated, we both signed on to work in management roles at my parents' restaurants.

"My mother and father told me almost daily that Ronald was going to make the perfect husband. A nice, normal human. Didn't matter that I had trouble saying why I wanted to be with the man. All that mattered to him or my parents was that we continued dating. Then, one night, I sat down to eat with Ronald and my parents, and after the salad course, my boyfriend told them he thought a fall wedding the following year would be the next best step."

The longer Neri speaks, the less emotion there is in her voice until she resembles a robot. But maybe the dry delivery is the only way she can finish this story.

"Mind you, this was the first I heard about any kind of wedding or engagement, and when I stopped the three of them in the middle of their planning to point this out, Ronald patted my hand like I was a good little girl"—her voice cracks there —"and told me that this made sense. That we fit together just fine. That our parents had known we would, which was why they had encouraged him to ask me out in the first place."

A muscle tics in her jaw, and I have to battle the urge to gather Neri into my arms as she opens this emotional wound in front of me.

"That was a shock. That even the start of our relationship had been a calculated move. That no one thought I needed to be consulted on the next steps in my life." She lets out a harsh, unamused laugh. "Like I'm an object that should stay in the place where I *fit*."

The story enrages me on Neri's behalf but also spurs a wild wave of panic. She's slipping away from me fast just when I got smart enough to know I need her.

"That was fucked up," I admit. "But that's not what we are, Neri. What's between us feels right. Being together would be so easy." The moment the words are out of my mouth, I know they were the wrong ones.

She snatches her car keys off the side table and jabs the air with one to emphasize each point she makes. "I don't want to be with someone because my parents or the gods are telling that person they should be my partner. I don't want the selling point of my relationship to be that it's convenient. Life isn't always easy. If I'm going to commit to someone, I need to know they'll fight for me, even when times get hard. And a man who is only reluctantly with me is not that man."

Even though she doesn't speak them aloud, her fierce glare adds the final heart-piercing words.

You are not that man.

The echo of the unspoken statement taints my home long after Neri leaves.

25

NERI

Sirens and witches have overrun Coffee & Claws.

The mass of mythics moves around the small shop with wild energy and devious intent in their eyes. Not that the coffee shop is at risk of their machinations. This is simply the final meeting of the Galen's Gauntlet planning committee. Tomorrow, construction starts, and the Gauntlet will take place in a few short days.

I should be excited.

Instead, I grit my teeth as I fight off a stress-induced headache that isn't helped by the zero hours of sleep I got last night. But I guess that's what happens when my anxious mind can't stop cycling back and forth between erotic memories and devastating images of Seamus's crestfallen face, followed immediately by my fury when I remember just why we can't be together.

This is a *him* problem.

I'm just the one smart enough to spot the detrimental fallout prior to us becoming too attached.

Issue is, I might be in deeper than I thought.

"Are there any fresh bear claws? I love when they're straight out of the oven." Aliyah, a siren who lives a few houses down from Sonya, bats her beautiful brown eyes at me.

Any other day, I'd be happy for a flirt from the gorgeous woman. Today, I can barely plaster on my customer-service smile with the color of her irises reminding me of a certain selkie's gaze. I probably look like someone stabbed me in the foot and I'm attempting to power through the pain.

"I'll check."

Sonya is here, so it's not a problem if I step away from the counter. Any excuse to get out of the lively front of the café. When I'm in the kitchen, my ears get a temporary break from the unrelenting chatter.

"Hey, Heath. Any claws ready soon?"

The bear sets down the cupcake he was icing and fixes a set of ice-blue eyes on me.

The scrutiny is not welcome.

"What?"

"Your vibe"—he gives a general wave at my entire body—"is tainting the kitchen. The dough will come out wrong."

"Seriously?" I choke on the word, pretty sure I should be insulted. "You're claiming my vibe will affect the taste of the food?"

The bear glares at me. "Yes. Go take your break. Meditate or something."

"Fine," I mutter, hating how petulant I sound. "Aliyah is at the counter and wants the claws. I'll be back in fifteen with a better *vibe*." Every bit of will I have goes to not stomping out the back door but instead walking in a mature, measured pace.

I save the sulky stalking for the parking lot, where I'm out of view. The sun lingers high, baking into the asphalt as I cross to the cool shade of the forest. When I reach the picnic table, I plop my ass down on the top and then immediately rocket back up at the thought of how similar the surface feels to the desk Seamus took me on yesterday.

"Damn The Winged One's tricks," I mutter, pacing around the table.

My body wants to move, but simple walking doesn't help much.

My shoulder blades itch. My wings want out.

Yesterday, a dam cracked. All the want that had been safely stored behind a thick concrete wall of denial was finally provided a moment of passage, and now, I can't brick things back up.

I want to fly.

And I want to fuck.

And I want ... more.

"Neri?"

The familiar voice sets off a tornado of emotions in my chest, but like with my itchy wings, I keep them all stuffed just below the surface as I turn to face him.

Seamus stands between two trees, his focus locked on me.

"What are you doing here?" I'm proud at my emotionless delivery and lack of reaction to his cringe.

"I was at the gas station when I saw you head this way. I wanted to talk to you." He steps closer, and somehow, his teasing scent reaches me, surrounding me with warm clay and fresh water.

"Everything that needed to be said was said." I hold my ground as he approaches.

"You're mad." Seamus stops a foot away, and I thank the gods he doesn't reach for me because I don't think I'd leave the circle of his arms if he did.

I shouldn't want this man.

"I'm fine." The lie rings out in the snappish way I answer.

"What can I do, Neri?"

"Accept that I'm not the one for you."

"Not like this," he growls, stepping closer, into my space.

I glare up at him. "You think you can make me? You going to call down the gods and beg them to turn me into your well-behaved puppet?"

Seamus's scowl matches mine. "I don't want a puppet. I want the siren with magnificent wings that rode me like I belonged between her legs."

A stroke of pleasure licks over my nerve endings at his description, and I briefly lose control of my body. Next thing I know, my arms hug his neck, my legs circle his waist, and my lips fuse to the selkie's. His groan vibrates against my tongue while he sinks onto the bench of the table with me straddling him.

While I plunder Seamus's mouth, his hand lands on my jean shorts and then slips lower, between my legs. The seam of the denim presses against my clit as his fingers ease into the leg opening, past the elastic of my underwear, discovering the slick lips of my pussy.

"Gods," he murmurs between my frantic kisses. "You're soaked for me."

Before I can respond, he presses two fingers inside me, and I choke on a sob of pleasure. My hips rock into his touch, silently asking for what I won't speak out loud. When the pleasure grows too sharp for my body to do anything but feel, I bury my face against his neck.

Unfortunately, that leaves his mouth free to talk.

"This is how things could always be. Between us. Be my m—"

I shove off his lap, cutting off his words—and my pleasure—and I land in an inelegant heap on the ground because I didn't manage to fully unwrap my legs before I tried to dismount. He can bet when I get up, I'm pissy as hell and ready to rip a selkie head off.

"No." With brutal smacks to my own ass, I try to get the dirt off my shorts, mortified I'll now be returning to work dirty, horny, and pissed off.

Heath is not going to approve of my vibe.

Seamus meanwhile gazes at me with stark longing that does unfair things to my already-frazzled mind. "Why won't you even give us a chance?"

"Because that's just setting myself up to get crushed!" I make sure to keep at least ten feet between us this time. My body won't let me forget the pressure of his fingers moving inside me. I need to focus. "What assurance do I have that if we get into an argument, you won't panic? That you won't think you're another version of Ginger, blindly following your inter-pretation of the gods' dictates to your own detriment? It was hard enough, getting rejected by you before, when I didn't—" I cut myself off just in time.

But Seamus catches on to the broken sentence with a wild light in his eyes. "When you didn't what?"

Of course. Of course this man wants everything from me.

Anxiety builds in my chest until I fear I might explode from the need to scream the truth. Tear myself open and expose raw nerve to reveal exactly why I can't let him any closer. So, I give him what he wants, only I sing this time.

"When I didn't love you."

I don't bother with a rhyme or even a full verse. Just that single honest line that reveals far too much. I'm not sure when or how it happened, but last night, lying awake in my bed with tears streaking across my cheeks, I silently admitted the truth to myself.

This will be the only time I admit how close to the sun I've flown, and then we can erase the memory together.

Seamus's mouth drops open, his shock apparent and expected. I wait for the glaze of forgetfulness to fog over his eyes.

It doesn't.

Too late, I recall the one loophole in siren-song amnesia. Maybe if I hadn't spent decades of my life pretending I was human, I wouldn't have so easily forgotten the rules of my kind.

My mother was right. A single slip is enough to endanger me. Only I don't think she had my heart in mind.

The selkie's voice vibrates deep in my bones when he next speaks.

"You love me?"

26

───────

NERI

"You weren't supposed to remember that!" I stumble back a step as Seamus rises slowly from his seat, wild brown gaze locked on me.

"You love me." He doesn't frame it as a question this time. He knows. Because I couldn't help verbalizing the truth this once.

But that's all it was supposed to be. Once.

Seamus approaches, slow but determined, and I now know what it's like to flee from a zombie in a horror movie.

"Stop!" A desperate note cracks through my shout, and—praise The Winged One—he stops.

"Neri—"

"I don't trust you," I hiss. "I can't be with you. I don't want to love you. Find a way to forget what I sang because it doesn't change anything."

Seamus closes his eyes, as if my words pained him.

Well, he pains me. Standing here in front of me, everything I want and yet all wrong for the job.

"I won't ever be able to forget it," he says, his voice low like the rumble of thunder in the distance.

"Then, learn to live with it. I have work." With a bracing breath, I turn.

But this selkie can never let things go.

"Will you come back to the library? Ever?"

A sharp ache goes through my chest when I think about that beautiful room. A place I felt at home for the first time in a long time.

But that's *his* place.

"I don't see how I can," I say to the trees, no longer able to shoulder the burden of his sorrowful expressions. Then, I walk away. Not run even though my body wants to, if only to escape.

When I get back to Coffee & Claws, I circle around to the front entrance, knowing if I go through the kitchen, the bear shifter will get on my case again. Maybe even send me home. But I need to work to get my mind off the selkie and his books.

At least the massive gathering of Gauntlet planners keeps me busy. I'm making my fiftieth latte of the day, carefully crafting a leaf design in the foam, when I glance up to find Sonya behind the counter, watching me.

"Why don't you take a break?" My cousin takes the coffee from my hand and passes it to the waiting customer.

"I just took one." *And it didn't go well*, I silently add.

"I know. That was three hours ago."

Really? Guess I got into the zone better than I thought. All the more reason not to leave it.

"I'm good."

Sonya moves behind me and sets her hands firmly on my shoulders. "You're coming with me. Heath! Man the front!" she calls out to her business partner through the pass as she lovingly shoves me away from my station.

"Where are you taking me?" The pout is back in my voice as we step into the heat of the day.

"Not far." Sonya turns us to the right and walks about twenty feet before stopping. "Here we go."

I glance around, but there's no bench or anything to take the load off my sore feet. Not a good break spot, in my opinion.

"What do you think?" Sonya asks.

"Of what?"

"This." She waves at the abandoned storefront beside us.

Confused, I examine the dusty glass and peeling painted sign that identifies the space as once having acted as a shoe repair shop.

"It's abandoned." I have no idea what answer she's searching for.

"Not anymore! I just bought it."

"Because you want to repair shoes now?"

Sonya digs a gentle elbow into my side. "Of course not. I bought this because I want to expand Coffee & Claws."

"Oh." I take another look at the storefront, glancing between it and the café. "That's cool. I'm glad you're doing well enough to expand." Despite my emotions twirling around in a roiling mess, I'm able to drum up enthusiasm for her new venture. And even if I can't figure out what my dreams are, it's good to watch someone I love achieve theirs.

"See, the thing is, I don't want to just have more seating for the café. I thought that we could use this space to start another business that's symbiotic with Claws."

"We?" I tuck my hands in my shorts and try not to remember the last set of fingers that explored underneath the frayed denim. "You mean, like you and Heath?"

"No. Like me and you." Sonya hits me with a grin so bright that I have to blink her cheer from my eyes before she burns my retinas. "I'm thinking a bookstore."

The world keeps existing around me, but for a moment, I am separate. Frozen outside of time as I try to make sense of the simple sentence. When I come back online, Sonya is still talking.

"College students sometimes study in the café, but a lot come and then leave. I bet they'd rather hang out in a bookstore. And you were lamenting Folk Haven's book situation just the other day. Really, I think this could be perfect. So, what do you say? Want to run a bookshop for me?"

"This ..." Where did my words go? My mouth garbles over them as I force a response out. "Too much. You can't do this for me."

Her lips twist. "You're not interested?"

Not interested? This is all I never knew I wanted.

"That's not the point." A sudden pressure of tears behind my eyes has me shaking my head to drive them away.

"Then, what, Neri?" Sonya wraps a supportive arm around my shoulders. "I thought you'd love the idea. What's the matter?"

I suck in a shaking breath, and then the truth bursts out with my exhale. "I don't get it."

"Don't get what?"

"Why you would do something so massive for me. Buying property for a business you don't even know if I can run?"

"First off, you ran your parents' restaurant for years, so I know you have a head for business." Sonya swipes a thumb under my eye, clearing away a tear that escaped. "But more than that, you have to know by now what I'm like. What being a siren in Folk Haven is like. We share things. Help each other. My guess is, something else is bothering you."

Sonya's words strike a chord of truth in my heart. Instead of retreating from the uncomfortable prodding, I embrace it. Dive deeper into myself, speaking as I work through my emotions.

"This feels ... like my parents. Like when they tried to give me the restaurant to run forever. No, wait." I wave my hands, rocking back as if that'd delete my previous conclusion. "This *looks* like that. So, I think I should feel the same way I did then. But I don't. That's what I don't get."

Sonya stares down at me, her brown eyes warm. "Did you want to manage a restaurant?"

"No. Never."

"Do you want to run a bookstore?"

I gasp in a steadying breath. "I do. So badly."

"Then, the answer is that simple. You want one thing and not the other." My cousin speaks as if nothing else needs to be said.

"But me leaving wasn't just about the restaurant," I press. "I was a puppet with my parents. None of the choices were mine. Every step of my life was a mapped-out path."

Sonya nods. "They made your choices easy because they made them all for you."

"Yes. Exactly."

"And the choice to run this bookstore seems easy." Her strong hand rubs my shoulder. "And that scares you."

"I ..." Clarity washes over me then. "Yes."

The corner of her mouth tilts up. "We're getting somewhere now. Let me reframe this for you." She pulls me closer for a one-armed hug. "You don't have to run the shop."

If she meant to put me at ease, she failed. Because I *want* to run the bookshop.

"I—"

"Wait. I'm not done. You don't have to run the bookshop for me to love you. If you turn me down, no big. I'll brainstorm other ways to use this space. And I'll keep helping you find your place in Folk Haven. But what I want us to be clear on is, this is an option, not a requirement."

Her words penetrate my anxious brain. If I turn Sonya down, I won't have to leave, like I did with my parents. This isn't a bargain for her love and acceptance. This is just an opportunity she thought I'd like.

And, gods, do I like this.

"It still seems too easy," I whisper, guilt twisting my stomach as I continue to hesitate when my cousin is hand-delivering me a perfect dream.

Sonya tilts her head back and forth before answering. "I think you need to realize there are different types of easy. There's easy because it's convenient for you and the people around you. That was you running the restaurant. Not rocking any boats or deviating from preplanned paths. But then there's another kind of easy. Easy because you know in your bones that it's right. And, Neri, you running a bookshop in Folk Haven just seems right, don't you think?"

Her profound wisdom sets off a flutter of excited wings in my chest.

"It does," I admit.

But my mind suddenly veers away from books.

Being with Seamus seemed easy. Too easy.

So easy that I told myself the whole thing would fall apart at the lightest breeze of doubt.

But what if Seamus is easy like a bookshop?

27

______

DELTA

I MUTTER a curse as my claw cracks another computer key. The third this week.

That's what happens when a dragon uses technology designed for delicate human fingers. The engineers obviously didn't consider that they might have an audience with claws tough enough to puncture concrete.

Doesn't help that I've been exchanging terse—on the verge of pissy—emails with my department head. Not for the first time, he's trying to force online faculty to follow the exact same teaching plan as in-person instructors. As if there were no difference between the learning styles.

What really has my palms burning is that he had a meeting to discuss this.

In person.

All of us remote faculty just got the meeting minutes and the final decision that was made without our input. I'm fucking tired of being considered second class because I've never breathed the same air as the guy.

Maybe I should have an actual conversation with Seamus about working at Ramla University. He seemed to think the institution would be excited about online courses aimed at serving a mythic community.

"Hey, Delta. I've got your order." The lyrical voice draws me away from dark thoughts about my job but not my curious ones about Seamus as I meet the silver gaze of the siren he's twisted up about.

"Thanks, Neri." I fold up my laptop and tuck it in my bag before accepting the coffee and scone I had to order over the phone as opposed to walking into the café like any other day. "Looks wild in there."

Neri glances toward the glass front of Coffee & Claws, where we can see animated discussions between what must be a good portion of the siren and witch population of Folk Haven.

"Yeah. I guess this Gauntlet thing is a big deal. Sorry if you're looking to pump me for insider info." Neri shrugs. "I'm so out of the loop. Figured my first year here, I should just watch."

"Right there with ya. I'll be in the audience." I raise my cup in a commiserating toast. "I'll just cheer for the selkies that enter."

Neri's blonde brows dip. "Not the dragons?"

"Hmm. No, I don't think so. I mean, I'm not friends with the other one in town. Yet. I've been meaning to introduce myself. But the MacNamaras kind of adopted me when Calder and I got together, and they're ..." *How do I explain the massive amount of love the selkie family heaped on me without making them sound smothering?*

"They're what?" Neri doesn't meet my gaze, but I get the sense she's hooked on the fishing line of my dangling sentence.

"They're more of a family than I ever expected to have." That sounds exactly right. "I guess I'm the kind of person who needs to collect people slowly, so I don't get overwhelmed."

Collect people. That wording would have frightened me in the past. Would have made me think I was falling into bad dragon hoarding habits. But now, I know better.

"That makes sense." Neri offers a small, distracted smile, and I take in her disheveled appearance.

The mythics must be running her nonstop inside. Better leave her to it.

"Well, I—"

"Neri, dear." A woman steps out of Coffee & Claws, focusing on the barista. The new arrival lets out a *click, click, click* as she walks, her yellow peep-toed heels making themselves known on the sidewalk. The vocal footwear pairs perfectly with her white-and-yellow polka-dot sundress, cut in a 1950s housewife style.

Pamela Townsend's signature style.

On any other woman, I would admire the adorable outfit for the simple fashion choice it is. Problem is, I'm pretty sure Pamela wears clothing from seventy years ago because she wishes the world would return to that era.

No, thanks.

"Pamela." Neri pastes on a customer-service smile. "Can I help you?"

"Well, I am sure you remember my order and that you will get around to it when you do." Her smile is as bright as the colors of a poisonous tree frog.

"Heath is working on your salad now," Neri replies with just as much artificial sweetness.

"Of course he is. Anyway, I just came out here to check on you." Pamela steps forward with another *click* that carries a warning. "You are new, so you might not know that people can be downright duplicitous when the Gauntlet approaches." Her eyes, blue as the water pirates sail their deadly boats on, flick to me and then away. "Best you stay around your own kind. In fact, I recommend that as common practice. Too much mixing just muddies the water, you know?"

Great. Just what I want to deal with today. Some judgment about my romantic relationship, disguised as sage advice.

When I first got together with my selkie, I thought my only worry would be protecting him from the strange skeletal creature that tried to steal his pelt on the night of the dark moon. But I haven't seen that thief again. On the other hand, I can barely go a day without getting a sneer or snide comment from mythics like Pamela. I'm starting to reevaluate my definition of dangerous.

"She's right," I say to Neri, causing Pamela to blink, as if my agreement slapped her across the face. But I'm not done. "Calder and I are terribly filthy when we're together. Downright dirty. I mean, can you imagine the possibilities when a man can hold his breath for *hours*?" I fight to keep my voice innocent as the stuck-up siren glares holes in my head. "Let's just say, despite the muddy waters you might have to swim through, I highly recommend a selkie mate."

As Neri's false smile melts into a real one, I silently pat myself on the back.

You're welcome, Seamus.

My job done here, I carefully pick up my other bag. But despite my gentle movements, I still disrupt the occupant, who lets this be known by poking her head out the top.

"Oh gods!" Pamela shuffles back, almost losing a heel in the process. "Your rat!"

I try not to let steam drift from my hands as I tamp down my anger. "As I've told you before, Pamela, Gigabyte is a dog. A well-behaved one." Especially when compared to uppity mythics who feel the need to comment on topics that don't concern them.

"Of course," she sneers. "How good of you to adopt that

pitiful creature." She grasps the handle to reenter the café but can't leave before one final comment. "Bless your heart."

Southern woman for *fuck you.*

"Yeah, right back at you," I call out in my flat Northern tone that has zero Southern drawl but plenty of snark to make up for it.

Neri dips her hand into her apron pocket and comes out with a small dog biscuit. "Almost forgot. Heath gave me this for Gig. Is it okay if I give it to her?"

"Go ahead."

The barista crouches down and offers my Chihuahua mutt the dry cookie, which she snatches up and then chews awkwardly on one side of the mouth because my beauty is missing half her teeth.

"Cutie." Neri stands, wiping crumbs off on her shorts. "Does that happen a lot? People saying things like Pamela did?"

Done with thinking about the condescending words, I want to shrug the whole topic off. But I know it's important to talk about. That's the first step in getting people to acknowledge the problem.

"Not everyone, or even the majority, feel that way. But there is a faction, and they aren't on the outskirts. And they're definitely not the quiet type."

Pamela is married to the town doctor.

"They judge quick and without asking questions. I mean, the whole prejudice arises from mixed mythic couples having offspring. That the kid would be an unknown factor. Calder and I talked, and we don't want kids. They just aren't a priority for us. I got myself a top-of-the-line IUD. So, poof, there goes the danger. Not that I'm saying the bigoted behavior is acceptable in other cases, but it just goes to show that they aren't driven by logic. Just fear and outdated ways of thinking." I suck in a deep breath and make sure my glasses are in place, betting my eyes have started to glow from the passion I feel about the topic. Luckily, the glass of my spectacles is spelled to hide the magical shimmer. "And now, I think I'll step off my soapbox and let you get back to your job."

Neri grins. "I don't mind a soapbox or two. Just … I don't think like Pamela. I want you to know. I'd like to be friends. Maybe with Calder too."

The hesitation over her tacked-on final sentence doesn't offend me. My guess is that Calder being Seamus's brother is the cause rather than his mythic species.

"I'd like that. I'll see you tomorrow for my next fix. We can plan a time to hang out. Maybe go to Local Brew," I say, naming the main bar in Folk Haven.

I waggle my coffee in good-bye, sharing a smile with the siren, and then take my bug-eyed dog to my car, so we can find another place to work for the day.

I end up in my Airstream.

The refurbished trailer used to be my home, but once I moved in with Calder, we parked the silver beast on a piece of land between his small cabin and his parents' expansive home-stead. I lucked out because, now, when I glance up from my screen, I'm treated to an unparalleled view of Lake Galen.

Gigabyte hops out of her bag and trots over to her little dog bed cave, falling asleep as I dive back into my work, typing very carefully this time.

I'm not sure how much time passes, but one moment, I'm in the midst of reformatting lesson plans, and then the next, my eyes are scratchy, my lower back aches, and a heavy set of hands lands on my shoulders. The thick fingers dig into knots that re-form every time I bend over my keyboard for too long.

"Oh gods," I groan, leaning backward against the wall that is Calder's body. "Don't stop."

"Never," he murmurs, pressing a kiss to the crown of my head. And the amazing thing is that he doesn't.

Many men would start a massage with the aim of getting

their partner just relaxed enough that they could cop a feel. But my selkie mate is determined to annihilate the ache in my shoulders, caring more for my comfort than his pleasure.

Some days, I wonder what I did to deserve such love and devotion.

But I try not to question my luck too often. Don't want the gods deciding to take it all away.

"How was work?" I ask in a melted-butter voice, every part of me turning to liquid under his strong kneading.

"Good. Had two scuba classes."

His firm touch drags down my arms, scooping up both my hands so he can massage them too. I gasp as the delicate, overused muscles receive his attention.

"Run into any half-naked women?" I smirk as I remember the first encounter I had with my mate. Took some time, but I finally got over the embarrassment of that scantily clad meeting.

A chuckle rumbles from Calder's chest through my back, where we're connected. "Would like to arrange that again. Next time, I'll send you the coordinates. Drop in whenever the mood hits."

Turning my chin, I give his bicep a playful bite. There's a twitch against my spine and then a slow hardening.

"Where would you like a massage next?" he asks, voice tight, even as he gently works the base of my thumb.

I could name anything. My feet, and he'd be on the ground in a second, digging his knuckles into my arches. But I want him on his knees for a different reason.

Taking control of his hand, I guide his fingers south until we reach the apex of my thighs. "Here."

Next thing I know, my selkie lover has me in his arms, walking the two steps it takes to get from my desk to the bed. He tosses me on the mattress as I laugh uncontrollably. This is what happens when my body has too much happiness to contain.

"I need to taste my dragon." Calder's skilled hands untie the floppy bow on the front of my linen shorts and tug the fabric off, lacy boy shorts along with them.

The *shirt and no shorts* look has always seemed a little ridiculous to me, but when Calder locks his hungry gaze on my vulva, I stop judging my outfit.

"Been starving all day," he mutters, kneeling on the floor of the trailer, putting himself at the perfect height to bury his face between my legs. Which he does, groaning in supplication.

I'd like to think I'm a generous lover, but in this moment, I'm pure selfishness. His hot breath teases my curls, and then his talented tongue strokes over my sensitive lips. Calder stimulates every part of me before finally kissing my clit. Then sucking it. Then pressing the heavy surface of his tongue against it.

"That's it. Just like that, baby." I urge him on with words, my nails scraping through his unruly curls and my legs pretzeling around his neck.

In the beginning, I worried about smothering him, but my mate told me about his magical lung capacity and how he wanted me to demand everything from him when he licked my pussy.

I wasn't lying to that stuck-up siren. The bitch is probably just jealous with her unimpressive human husband.

Calder digs his fingers into my ass, leaving the bruises I love to make him kiss the next morning. Pleasure burns up my spine until I'm bowing off the bed, drawn tight. Needing just one snap to set me free. The release comes when Calder sinks three fingers inside me, curling them in a beckoning motion as he sucks my clit like hard candy.

Mythics have never agreed upon the lore for what happens

after we pass away, but I hope my afterlife is this. A perfect twining of love, pleasure, and connection.

When I blink the fog of the post-orgasm haze out of my eyes, my selkie hovers above me, joy and self-satisfaction illuminating his face.

"Enjoy your happy ending?"

Cocky, adorable bastard.

"You say that like we're done." Pulling on the strength of my dragon, I wrap a leg around his waist and flip him onto his back.

"Delta," he groans as I grind down on the hard length in his khaki shorts.

A second later, I have his fly down and his cock in my hand.

"When you give me a massage"—I use my instructor voice —"I need you to go deep." As I speak the last word, I slide him inside me, luxuriating in the stretch and his choked gasp of pleasure.

As I ride slow and relentlessly, Calder leaves more delicious fingerprints on my skin.

Meanwhile, I leave claw marks on his.

Later, we lie, panting and sated, twined together in a mess of sheets and half-removed clothes. The only thing that gets me moving is my throat, dry from calling out my mate's name.

"Water," I mutter as I slide away from him.

My selkie lets his palm linger on the curve of my ass as I rise, and I revel in his need to touch. To connect.

My life was lonely before I found a place in Folk Haven.

The sun is still above the trees when I glance out my window toward the lake. The occasional boat motors through the wide channel as I chug half my water bottle. Glancing toward the MacNamaras' dock, I spy a body floating.

Not a dead body, I assure myself with a wry smile.

Squinting my eyes, I make out the familiar figure.

"Seamus is swimming." I settle into Calder's side and hand him my water bottle.

His face grows contemplative as he takes a few swallows. "He's been distracted lately. More than usual."

The academically inclined MacNamara sibling often has his attention half somewhere else. I can't imagine what a distracted Seamus is like. Probably wandering into the middle of a busy road.

"I saw Neri today. You think it's something to do with her?"

Calder gazes down at me, his attention piercing deep into my soul. "I couldn't concentrate on anything else when I first found you. Still holds true most days."

"Sweet-talker." Despite the tease in my voice, I fall even more in love with my mate in this moment, pressing a long kiss to the skin above his heart. "As much as I want to hide you away in this trailer forever, maybe you should go talk to him. Help him out."

Calder captures my mouth for a languid, long kiss that melts my body all over again.

"Fine," he grumbles, even as he smiles against my lips.

"Take Gig with you." I gesture toward the dog peeking out of her hidey-hole. "She's a good comfort dog. Also, she needs to go to the bathroom."

"Yes, Professor Novac." He salutes me as he stands and then grabs my ankle, dragging my squealing body toward him so he can lean over and plant a loud, smacking kiss on my bare ass.

I'm still laughing when he pushes my trailer door open, Gig cradled in his arms. At the sound of the other MacNamara brother's voice, I hurriedly pull a sheet over my naked body.

"Look at you and your shit-eating grin." Owen's mocking drifts to me through the trailer walls. "Someone just got laid. Hussy."

"Shut up," Calder replies without heat. "You see Seamus down there?"

"Yeah. Mama called 'cause she saw him moping. I'm on a mission to make sure he doesn't drown himself. You my backup?"

"Yep. Think we need Moira too?"

I can imagine Owen giving one of his signature lazy shrugs. "Let's save her as a plan B."

Their voices fade, leaving me alone in my blissful state. Sometimes, I have trouble believing how happy I am. So much so that I'm tempted to sabotage something just to prove that this can't be real. Luckily, I found a good therapist who knows about mythics, and she helps me to keep from breaking this precious, amazing thing I've found.

Maybe I should find a way to recommend her to Neri. I don't know what is coming between the siren and Seamus, but I've decided I want others to discover what it's like to be loved by a MacNamara. And I wouldn't mind an ally on occasion.

A lovingly evil grin curls my lips as I imagine all the ways we could shake up the selkie siblings.

28

———

SEAMUS

THE WATER CRADLES my body as the sun bakes the exposed skin on my chest. With my ears below the surface, sound becomes a solid din of white noise that helps calm my nerves. This whole experience of floating helps me achieve a meditative state, where I can briefly forget the turbulence in my life.

Exist as the water does. Calm. Uncaring. No heart to break. The water doesn't long for anything. The water simply is.

"Cannonball!" The shout barrels into my Zen state a moment before a wave swamps me, and I lose my grip on a blank mind.

When I surface, I'm snorting Lake Galen from my nose and staring into the unrepentant eyes of my most annoying brother.

"Hey, pouty-pants. We're here to make sure you don't drown." Owen smirks in the face of my glare.

Scoffing at the ridiculous notion of a selkie drowning, I glance toward the dock and discover both of my brothers have ambushed me. Calder sits on the dock, his feet dangling over the edge and disappearing into the water.

173

Preferring his company over Owen's, I heave myself out of the lake and plant my ass on the sun-bleached wood next to him, taking silent pleasure in knowing the puddle forming around my seat will creep its way over to him, soaking his shorts.

So what if I'm a respectable professor with a PhD? All that maturity evaporates when I'm near these two demons.

Then, I notice the small creature in Calder's lap. "Can that thing even swim?"

My baby brother levels me with a reprimanding stare. "Gigabyte is a dog. And you say anything disparaging about her within Delta's hearing, my mate will rip your testicles off." He scoops up the animal that must be some sort of Chihuahua and offers the wide-eyed thing to me. "Besides, Delta sent her down with me when she saw you moping."

Over Calder's shoulder, I spy the Airstream my sister-in-law set up on an empty plot of land next to my parents' house at their encouragement. The broad window on the side has a clear view of Lake Galen and this dock.

I'm not particularly happy to find out my self-loathing was on display. But secretly, some part of me must have wanted to be discovered or else I would have gone swimming off my own dock rather than my parents'.

Calder continues to hold the bug-eyed animal in my face.

"What am I supposed to do with her?"

"Hold her, obviously." When I make no move in response, Calder gently arranges his mate's animal companion on my thighs, which are covered by a wet bathing suit that will soon have a generous coat of dog hair.

Fantastic.

Still, I'm not going to mistreat a dragon's pet.

Making a sort of bed with my arms, I gather the dog closer to my chest, suddenly worried that my question about swimming ability still hasn't received a definitive answer.

"This thing is shaking." With a single finger, I scratch behind her ears. "Is she about to detonate?"

Calder leans back on his hands, unconcerned with the situation. "That's just how Gig is."

"And her anxiety is supposed to soothe me? How exactly does that work?"

"It's a comparison thing." Calder grins. "You think you're stressed? Never as stressed as Gigabyte!"

"I don't like the idea of causing small animals distress for my own gain. Take her back." I hold out the quivering mess to my brother, but he waves me off.

"She'll calm down in a second. Just pet her while you tell us how you messed everything up with your barista."

"What? How did you ... I mean, I didn't." I clear my throat. "I don't know what you're talking about."

"You need to work on your lying." Owen offers an evil smirk from where he treads water in front of us. "Let's just skip the whole *denying everything* part and get to you telling us how you screwed up, so we can help you."

My first instinct is to snap back at my brother. That's how our relationship tends to work, exchanging barbs. But I find I don't want to fight.

I want to fix what went wrong between Neri and me.

"I drove away my mate," I admit.

The two silently take in my admission, and I focus on the slowly calming dog in my lap rather than trying to read their expressions.

"I thought you didn't want a mate," Calder says as if the words were a casual comment rather than a condemnation, which helps me push away my defensiveness.

"I didn't want a *fated* mate. But that doesn't matter anymore. I want Neri. And maybe Neri happens to be my gods-chosen mate. But I want her either way. I don't care if it's fate or biology or what. She's just ... perfection. To me."

Calder makes a grunt of agreement.

"Sounds nice," Owen offers as he floats by. "Where'd you go wrong?"

Even though the facts will give them plenty of fodder in the future for mocking me, I lay everything out. Well, everything, except for the details about hook-ups. They don't need to know that. I also talk about Ginger. Living in Folk Haven, Owen and Calder crossed paths with my friend and her human boyfriend. But they never knew what went on behind closed doors.

"Neri thinks I'll always compare our relationship to Ginger's. That I'll run if things don't constantly go smoothly between us. That I won't be willing to work on our relationship if I think the gods ordained it."

"This is rough right now," Calder points out. "But you're not giving up. Right?"

"Right," I growl. Maybe I'm not chasing after Neri at this exact moment, but I haven't given up. All I need is to figure out the way forward without making all this worse.

"When I didn't love you."

Her enchanting voice and those revealing words play through my head on a loop. How do I remember them? One day, that will be the important question. Right now, my main concern is convincing Neri to speak the words without the hope of me forgetting.

"So, shouldn't you showing up again prove you're in this thing?" Calder reasons.

"I already did. Only I think it made things worse." The words she spoke after her song still leave aching wounds in my chest. "Driving to where she works is easy. I don't think that'll prove much. I'm not leaving my comfort zone when I go to a coffee shop." I scratch Gigabyte under her chin, surprised to find she's stopped shaking. "I think I need to get uncomfortable. Prove I'll fight for us, to make up for my past panicked reactions. But there's no fortress to conquer or battle to win in her name."

Owen leans back in the water, eyes closed, evil grin on his face. "Yeah, there is."

29

———————

NERI

I EXPECTED Galen's Gauntlet to take place at night. Maybe under the shadow of the dark moon, the entire event hidden from the world. Or under the full moon, like the night the siren killed The Collector.

But no. The Gauntlet happens at noon on a Sunday.

"Those must be some powerful protection spells." I glance over at Sonya.

We sit side by side on a thick branch, garnering a perfect view of the festivities starting below. A massive crowd of people —I assume all mythics or at least humans who know about mythics—gathers along the shore. Some set up camping chairs. Some wear T-shirts with names on them. I even spot an air horn or two.

How much magic does it take to hide this many beings and all their celebrating?

"You bet your shit they are. That's why the witches get a fourth of the pot. They've been weaving the spells over this cove for weeks." Sonya stretches her wings out behind her, far enough that the sun falls on them. "Enjoy this freedom while you can. Only comes once every other year."

I follow suit, extending my own wings, groaning in delight at how glorious the sensation feels. The best stretch I've ever had. As I glance back to admire the view, my sight homes in on the splash of red.

A tradition Sonya showed me. On the day of Galen's Gauntlet, all sirens dip the tips of our wings in red paint, symbolizing the sacrifice our ancestor made. When she tore apart her wings to finally kill The Collector and save all he had imprisoned.

The vibrant splash of color instills a pride deep in my chest. Every day, I learn more about my history. Every day, I become more a part of this community.

Slowly, I'm finding my place.

"We seem to fit together."

Seamus's words rattle through my mind, knocking away the contentment. He wanted to offer me a place. One at his side.

Because I'm convenient, I remind myself.

Even though I need the reminder, it still hurts. Because a place beside Seamus started looking pretty good. Somewhere I'd want to be for a stretch of time. One without ending.

But how long before he got resentful of playing the game he saw placed forth by the gods? Would he stay even if things got hard? Would he put in the work?

A shout pulls me away from the memory of his devastated face. I welcome the distraction of the Gauntlet.

"What happens next?" I lean forward on my perch, eyeing the gathering near the opening of the inlet.

Multiple floating platforms are anchored just inside the mouth, and I watch as people swim out to them. A lot of people.

"The competitors assemble at the starting line. When they are all accounted for and have sworn to follow the rules or forfeit their place in the race, the starting horn will go off, and the fun will begin." Sonya rubs her hands together, all eager anticipation.

"So, there are rules to this thing?"

"Yeah. Zelda has the book with them all listed. A big one is no shifting is allowed. And competitors can't go on the banks. They must stay within the barriers of the water. Also, no spells."

"Are witches competing?"

Even without shifting, most mythics with secondary forms have added strength and stamina in their human shape.

Sonya shakes her head. "Not allowed since they joined forces with sirens to ward the place and build the obstacles. But there was a time when competitors bought spells prior to the Gauntlet and used them during the race. Things got bloody, and the winner was whoever had the deepest pockets, which didn't come off as fair. Hence the *no spells* rule."

Interesting. My curiosity grows, and I make a note to be part of the planning committee next time around, so I can have a better understanding of everything the competitors will face. For now, I scan the group entrants, satisfaction rising as I recognize faces of customers from the coffee shop.

This is a perfect time to make note of who I've come across that is also a mythic. We don't have any identifiers when out in public, so I'm only sure someone is magical when Sonya tells me. But here, everyone is part of our world. At least, among the competitors.

On the far end is a large Black man who always orders a cappuccino on Monday and tips well. If I remember correctly, his name is Xavier. I'm always better at connecting faces to orders rather than names, but I've worked in the shop long enough to have a few down.

Farther down the line is a group of men shotgunning beers. I have no idea who they are, and I don't have a lot of hope for their *get drunk* strategy. But what do I, a Galen's Gauntlet newbie, know?

There are two women in full-body wet suits, also wearing swim caps, facing each other, so I can't figure out if I've seen them before or not.

A woman named Tanvi stands beside them, her thick black hair restrained in a tight French braid that pulls the russet skin of her forehead taut, and I wonder how she's doing without the double-shot café au lait she orders every morning. Coffee & Claws is closed for the day, so regulars had to find their own caffeine.

What type of mythic could she be? Is it rude to ask?

Growing up in the human world, I don't know what is and is not accepted among my kind. Sometimes, I worry I bother Sonya with my unending questions. Like she's raising a toddler.

I decide to save my queries until later, after the excitement of the race is over.

Trailing farther down the line, my attention snags on a devastatingly handsome man with flowing black hair that brushes his chin. His skin holds the barest tan, and his nose is almost too prominent, yet it somehow works on his face. He's come into Coffee & Claws a handful of times but not enough for his name to have stuck. Flavored coffee, oat milk, and cocoa powder. I remember that much at least. He bends his head to talk to the person on his left. When I catch sight of the one capturing his focus, I stutter on my breath.

Moira MacNamara.

"What trick of The Winged One?" I mutter.

The realtor has on a one-piece bathing suit, and she tamed her wild curls in a braid similar to Tanvi's. The selkie stares over the cove, even as the gorgeous man speaks to her. Despite the preparedness of the other competitors, I can't help thinking everyone's money should go on the selkie woman. She has an air of undaunted determination about her.

Then, all thoughts of Moira flee as I scan down the rest of the line and almost fall from my perch when I spy an even more familiar form. A body I know intimately.

Seamus MacNamara stands, ready to compete in Galen's Gauntlet.

"What the fuck?!" I yelp, leaping up to stand on the branch, getting a clearer view of the starting line.

But changing my angle doesn't alter the sight. It's him. The infuriating selkie nerd I can't get my vagina to shut up about.

"What's wrong?" My cousin stands beside me, trying to see whatever sent me yelling.

"Seamus is down there." I gesture with a wild wave. "Like a competitor!"

"Oh." Her tone is far less concerned than mine. "Must have been a late entry. What's wrong with him competing?"

How about because I love him?

But I don't say that out loud.

"Because he's a geek!" My reasoning lacks logic, but my brain isn't working at full capacity at the moment.

Sonya gives me a disbelieving look I deserve.

"So?"

"So, you said this thing is dangerous! He's a book guy. He belongs in the classroom. Not like ..." With a frustrated growl, I wave toward the beer shotgunners, who now appear to be passing around a flask.

Sonya snorts. "Yeah, well, the mermen usually have a particular prize in mind." She offers a snarky grin. "Winner drinks for free at Local Brew for the next year."

"And I'm sure that makes all this worth it to them," I growl. "But Seamus doesn't need to do this. Didn't you say the obstacles are a mindfuck? Haven't people died?"

"Not since the '80s. And the last time it happened was the guy's own fault. He found a sharp rock and decided to go after his competitors with it. Made the mistake of stabbing a werewolf. Not a good idea. The wolf shifted and ripped him to shreds." My cousin shrugs, as if that were something not to be concerned about.

"Are there any wolves competing this year?" I shouldn't ask, but my morbid curiosity gets the better of me.

Suddenly, the sketch of that bony creature creeps up from my memory. Could one of these competitors shift into that form? Is there someone here, looking to steal a selkie's skin? Or maybe just hurt them?

Sonya bites her lip, and with a sigh, she points at a white man halfway down the line. "Fred is in the Folk Haven pack." She shifts her finger to my double-shot café au lait regular. "Tanvi is also a member. Her father is the alpha."

At my cousin's grimace, I know there's more information.

"What aren't you telling me?"

"It's really no big deal."

"Then, tell me."

She rolls her eyes. "A few years ago, Tanvi competed and got trapped in one of the obstacles with another competitor. And she might have ... bitten his finger off. But he deserved it!" Sonya hurries the last statement out, as if that should somehow calm my nerves.

"Oh gods," I moan as my eyes seek out my bookworm selkie. "Why would he do this?"

In that moment, Seamus glances up. Across the distance, our eyes lock. His that warm liquid brown. Mine no doubt expressing every ounce of worry and frustration I have for him.

Then, he offers a slight smile and a nod of his head.

For me. He's doing this for me.

My stomach drops as if my wings failed me mid-flight. I brace myself to launch off the branch and dive down to pull him away from danger.

But before I can move, the starting horn cracks through the air.

30

———

SEAMUS

THE LOOK on Neri's face gives me hope. Concern. The siren met my eyes and seemed worried for me.

Maybe this wild plan could work after all. Enter myself in Galen's Gauntlet to prove I'm willing to get dirty and to fight for a chance at happiness. Taking part in a magical competition isn't the same as dealing with relationship hardships, but hopefully, Neri will think this is a good start.

Any chance I can find, I'll take.

That's why *I'm* putting myself through this hellish trial, but why is my sister here?

As the crowd roars, Moira plunges into the water ten feet away from me, a determined scowl on her face.

There goes any chance I had of winning.

When Moira wants something, she gets it. And not because the world hands it to her. My sister takes what she wants by having more drive than anyone around her.

Good thing my goal isn't to win. Sure, that would have been nice. An impressive showing in front of the siren I'm hoping to prove myself to. But I believe the act of competing, putting my all in to get as far as I can, will prove my point. Grind myself through every one of the dangerous, degrading situations. Even when I encounter pain, I'll push forward, showing Neri that I'm not the type to give up when things get uncomfortable.

That she can trust me not to give up on us.

But I shove thoughts of my siren to a far corner of my mind and concentrate. Focusing becomes easy when a massive wave of fire rolls across the surface of the water toward all of the competitors. Yelps fill the air, but the sounds immediately cut off when I dive below the surface.

This, at least, is an easy obstacle for me. I could stay immersed for hours. On the other hand, the need for oxygen drives the other competitors forward, many outpacing me. Embarrassing that a handful ahead of me aren't even water mythics. No doubt Owen will use this as inspiration for future mocking, even as he sits comfy on the sidelines. I kick my legs hard and use the slight ability I have to control the water around me to shoot forward, gaining so much speed that I almost plow straight into a chain-link fence. The metal barrier presses cold against my fingers.

Am I supposed to rise to the surface?

But when I gaze up, there's still flashing lights, hinting that the fire remains.

The fence quivers and shakes. Glancing to the sides, I realize others have found random breaks in the chain-link where they push themselves through. I spy a merman feet from me, already halfway to the other side. Like a crab in a trap, I scuttle sideways, seeking freedom. But my searching lacks the desperation of some because I just want to move forward while others are frantically seeking oxygen. Just as I'm about to reach the hole, a heavy foot slams into my chest. As bubbles burst from my mouth, I meet the glowing yellow gaze of Xavier, a dragon who lives in town. He smirks before disappearing through the opening.

Mythics came to play today. No making friends.

I follow after him and swim my way to the surface. Luckily, there's no fire threatening to singe my scalp when I break into the daylight. Around me, mythics pant for breath. I don't need that recovery time, so I keep swimming forward.

The way appears clear, but I'm not fool enough to believe the sirens and witches are done with their sneaky games. I flinch when my feet brush against something solid. Belatedly, I realize the water is shallow enough for me to stand chest deep. The inlet the sirens chose for the Gauntlet is odd in that way. Varying depths with large rocks randomly jutting out of the water. Not a good place to boat, but perfect for a risky race.

The shallow water has me worried I'm drifting too close to the shore. Stepping a foot on the banks means automatic disqualification. When I glance to the side, I find I have a good thirty feet of buffer space.

I should refocus on the game, but I can't help searching the branches for Neri. One quick sighting. Just a hint of her white-gold hair. But the midday sun shines bright in my eyes and casts everything under the trees in shadow. I lift my hand to shield my gaze.

My hesitation is a mistake.

A giant mass bludgeons my hand, and all sensation from my elbow to my fingertips disappears.

NERI

"What was that?" I fail to keep the panic out of my voice.

There's no blood. Just a strange green powder clinging to the skin of Seamus's forearm.

Sonya cackles as we watch another siren wing over the inlet and drop a cloth bag among the competitors. One of the tipsy mermen yelps and then stops moving entirely, his body bobbing, loose-limbed, on the surface. Spectators roar with laughter and approval.

"Paralyzing powder." My cousin takes a sip of her beer before explaining further. "See how they can't move whatever the powder touches? You lose control of that part of your body. But then that part floats." The cursing merman acts as an almost-academic demonstration. "See? We're not *trying* to kill anyone."

"It's not permanent, right?" I watch as Seamus powers forward through the water, dragging his useless arm behind him.

"Of course not. The effect will wear off in a few minutes. Hell of a speed bump but won't put you out of the game completely." Sonya stands on the thick tree limb, stretching her wings out. "Come on. Let's go find another seat."

"Really? We can move closer?"

Sonya grins at me. "Of course. Don't forget, this is *our* show. As long as you don't interfere with the race, you can get as close as you want."

Can I hover over Seamus the entire way? I don't ask the question out loud, no matter how much I want to become his protective cloud.

Instead, I leap off the tree branch a moment after my cousin, gliding with her farther down the inlet.

My wings devour the wind, stroking through the air currents in a loving caress. How did I let myself go so long without experiencing this integral part of myself? Every muscle in my body sings a euphoric melody at this new yet familiar stretch and pull.

I can never go back to the woman I was before. Only a fraction of my true self.

When I land on a branch just below Sonya's, I try not to wobble. My landings could use some work, but I plan on getting a lot more practice. We've come to a wider, deeper section of the inlet. This stretch has calm water and no signs of any obstacles.

"Do they get a break during this leg?" I ask.

Sonya smirks down at me. "Oh, sweetie. They don't get a break until someone wins. Or they tap out."

As Seamus swims forward with a powerful, one-armed stroke, I can't help gnawing on my nails. He's surrounded by other competitors, firmly in the middle of the pack. Is that good? Bad?

Probably the second. All of this is bad.

Just as I'm about to ask Sonya what the next challenge is, a metallic screech echoes over the water, followed closely by a reverberating clang. The sounds repeat, bouncing off of the trees and rocks until the air fills with the dreadful chorus, and I watch as contestants get swallowed by medieval-looking cages.

"What trick of The Winged One?" I whisper.

"Love cage!" my cousin crows.

More sirens take up the cry until the air reverberates with the gleeful chant. *"Love cage! Love cage! Love cage!"*

"What in all the gods' names is a love cage?" I yell over the din.

As I examine the traps from a distance, I'm relieved to realize that the metal cages aren't sinking back under the water once they've snagged their prey. A good portion of the trap sits below the surface, but there's enough space for heads to bob in the fresh air.

"They're a tribute to Galen's secret liaisons with her selkie lover," Sonya explains. "Legend has it, they found ways to break into each other's prisons, risking everything for one more night with their love."

"Oh. Uh, I guess that's sweet." The sentiment doesn't exactly translate as I watch Tanvi grip the bars of her cage and shake them with bared teeth. "How do they get out?"

Sonya doesn't have to bother answering my newbie question as another chant starts up. *"Kiss! Kiss! Kiss!"*

"Time for some soft-core porn!" a siren on a branch to my left bellows before launching into the air, gliding closer for a better view.

"You've got to be fucking with me," I growl, throwing a glare Sonya's way.

She shrugs with a teasing smile.

"It's only a kiss. They need to make friends fast with their fellow captive. One of the easier tasks, in my opinion."

Easy for *her*. She's not in love with one of the competitors. I frantically search the cages, trying to figure out which one Seamus is in.

But he's not. Instead, I spy him fighting his way between the cages. His moves appear more frantic than they should be. Like something has ahold of him.

Then, the selkie raises his non-paralyzed arm, and I spot something snakelike twisting around the limb.

"Enchanted ropes," Sonya offers before I ask the question. "Guess he's getting away without locking lips. Too bad for him. The cages wouldn't try to strangle him."

I mutter curses as I watch the rope twine around his chest and jerk him under the surface.

"He's going to drown!" I'm ready to dive off my branch after him, but Sonya grabs my wrist.

"He's a selkie. He can hold his breath underwater for hours."

Her words might pierce through to the logical part of my brain, but my panicked heart doesn't want to listen. My body aches to scoop him out of the water and fly him back to the safety of our library.

Seamus putting himself through all of this for me makes me sick.

But what other option did I leave him?

His head breaches the surface, and I gasp a breath of temporary relief. From the thrashing, I can tell he's still struggling. Then, I watch him tear the rope away, using his teeth. He pushes toward a cage, using both his hands to twine the rope through the bar. I don't know if the paralyzing powder was supposed to last longer or if he got an indirect hit. Whatever the cure, I'm just happy his body is fully functioning.

With a final tug, Seamus tightens the knot. The rope writhes like a thing possessed but stays tied down. That's when I realize the cage Seamus tied the rope to holds his sister and that dark-haired handsome man I spotted at the starting line. Moira looks to be in no mood to kiss the man as she tries to dig her fingers in the joints of the cage.

Refocusing on Seamus, I watch him approach a turn in the inlet. In a moment, he'll disappear from view. Leaping off my perch, I wing after him.

31

———

MOIRA

"Hey, sis," Seamus calls out before swimming away, leaving me to my fate.

So much for brotherly love. The rope he tied to my prison twitches in a furious rhythm, as eager to get free as I am.

"You know there's only one way to get out of this cage," Levi says behind me, his tone calm. Reasonable. Entirely unaffected. "We might as well get it over with."

As much as I loathe admitting the monster is right about anything, I know that unless I want to wait until the whole Gauntlet is over, I have one option. Even if we did wait till the end, the sirens might be masochistic enough to leave us in here until we fulfilled the requirement.

"Go for it, Moira!" The sound of my name and a familiar voice drag my attention to the shore, where a crowd mills. Owen stands at the edge of the water, grinning like a gator, his hands cupped around his mouth. "No one is watching! I swear!"

He's immediately proven a liar by the group of selkies

behind him, who let out a whoop of agreement. Mama steps up beside Owen and gives me an encouraging thumbs-up.

Curse the love cage and the twisted mind that created the obstacle.

Letting fury drive my movements, I whip around, glaring at the handsome, aggravating man.

"Fine," I hiss. Then, I lunge at him, grab his shocked face, and smash my lips onto his.

This is clinical. Two body parts touching. Nothing more, I remind myself as an almost-electrical force builds between us.

I have complete control of the situation until he groans. The needy, deep noise flows from Levi's mouth to mine, scalding my throat as the erotic response overwhelms my senses. Hard arms bracket my body, caging me as effectively as the bars around us.

Bad. This is bad. But also ... so good.

The restraint of his hold should piss me off. But I don't fight back. If anything, I surge closer, painting myself across the canvas of a man I swore I'd rather stab than kiss. My tongue tingles at the hint of salt on his lips. Where that spice comes from—when we've been swimming through fresh water—is a mystery to me. Still, I drink the monster down like he's the ocean I dream so often of sinking into. Levi might as well be the wild waters of the sea with how I slide so easily into everything he offers.

No. Not him. Don't give in to him.

The words struggle past the pleasurable dig of greedy fingers into wet skin. I'm lucid enough to know this is wrong but weak enough to keep kissing. Anger crashes through me at how much he's making me enjoy what should be a chore. Punishing him, I bite down on Levi's lip.

As the iron tang of blood coats my tongue, his cock hardens between us.

Another groan rattles the air around me, but this time, it's not from the beast in my arms.

The cage parts above us, and in a daze of lust, I stare up at Zelda's familiar face. The siren's musical voice holds a mocking note when she speaks.

"You lovebirds had better get a move on." She winks and then glides away.

Reality slams into me, cold as an arctic wave. I made out with a man I loathe. In front of my family.

Curse The Finned One's games.

I shove out of Levi's clutches, only meeting his midnight eyes briefly before plunging under the surface and swimming faster than I have my entire life on Lake Galen. All because of a single emotion I read with terrifying ease in his stare.

Possession.

32

NERI

JUST AROUND THE BEND, I discover the once-calm waters of Lake Galen have gone turbulent, disturbed by a string a whirlpools spanning from shore to shore. No way for anyone to get past them without climbing up on the shore and disqualifying themselves.

A siren hovers over each whirlpool, and I recognize them as the more reserved ladies I've been introduced to. The ones who clasp tightly to tradition. Pamela and her bunch. The siren herself holds claim to a whirlpool right in the middle of the pack.

A few other contestants have reached this obstacle before Seamus. One merman doesn't bother to acknowledge the siren hovering overhead, instead swimming directly into the whirlpool.

Mistake.

He's immediately caught in the twisting current, only to be flung out a moment later, skipping across the lake surface like a smooth stone thrown by a child. The guy's progress halts when an enchanted rope snatches him from the air.

The audience along the shoreline cheers at the display, but I'm more concerned with Seamus than watching other competitors get knocked around.

A werewolf—Fred, I recall Sonya calling him—takes the moment needed to converse with a siren I don't recognize, and I listen close.

"What burns but is not Of the Flame?" Then, with a haughty grin, she says the answer. "*A dragon.*"

No, wait. She doesn't say it.

She *sings* it.

The man in front of her goes glassy-eyed as he immediately forgets.

"Um ... just a second." The wolf shakes his head to clear that lingering dizziness as he tries to solve the puzzle.

Seamus paddles up to a siren not already conversing, and of course, it has to be Pamela, who looks perfectly put together in her immaculately ironed slacks, even as she hovers in the air with steady flaps of her wings.

"How do I get past?" he calls out.

"Simply solve this riddle." She clears her throat for dramatic effect. "What cannot sleep but needs to rest?"

Then, just like with the other competitor, she sings the answer, smirking at the selkie when the last note fades away.

Seamus frowns up at her. "Why'd you give me the answer?"

The confidence on the siren's face changes to confusion. "Excuse me?"

"I'm just saying, if you gave me a moment, I'm sure I could have solved it. But fine. The answer is *dough*. Did Heath come up with that riddle?"

"You remember what I sang?" Pamela asks, shock in her wide eyes.

"Yes. Now, may I pass? Please."

The siren gapes down at him, and then her blue eyes search the area, finally resting on me, where I watch closely how things are progressing with Seamus. Understanding mixes with a glare on her face. She mutters something that looks like *not right* but then dives down to dip a talisman in the frothing waters. Instantly, they calm, but Seamus doesn't move forward.

Instead, his attention follows the siren's previous path, his eyes finding their way to me. I know the moment he sees me because the selkie smiles wide and lifts a hand in a wave.

"Stop looking at me and get your ass in gear!" I holler. Who knows what challenge is up next?

Seamus drops his arm into the water and pulls ahead with a series of strong strokes.

Ignoring the judgment in Pamela's seething glare, I glide from branch to branch, following Seamus's advancement. At one point, he slows down, movements sluggish. Eyeing the other competitors, I find they're all going slow too. Something is up with the water. As spectators jog along the shore, repositioning themselves to observe those in the lead, I wonder if this slow-mo is truly an obstacle or maybe just an intermission so the audience can catch up.

A moment later, people start jutting forward, as if getting expelled from a Jell-O mold. But they don't charge ahead. The sight before them confuses even me.

Bubbles. Hundreds of massive bubbles.

The smallest is the size of my head, but they get as large as a golf cart. Bigger even.

And unlike the normal clear quality of soap bubbles, these are opaque and range the color spectrum. Blue, yellow, green, red, purple. There's even a handful of white ones.

The orbs float leisurely on the surface of the water, but some look to be partially submerged.

From the way Seamus and his competition have stopped pumping their arms, my guess is, they've reached the part of the inlet shallow enough to stand. Which means there's going to be no swimming underneath the obstacle.

"We've never had this challenge before. A new witch in town offered it as a tribute to Galen." The downdraft of Sonya's wings has me brushing hair from my face.

"What are they?"

"I'm not exactly sure. But the witch claimed her focus was in emotions. We'll both have to wait and see."

"You don't think they'll hurt, do you?"

Sonya fingers the red tip of her wing. "The core of this competition is to honor the siren who suffered to save our ancestors." Her eyes meet mine, the normally soft brown irises hardening. "A winner has never come out unscathed. Everyone who enters knows that."

But Seamus wouldn't have entered if he wasn't trying to prove something to me.

As if in silent agreement, everyone in the water moves forward at once. Speed has left the lake. Now, all their focus centers on careful maneuvering. The bubbles bob and float in the water, conveying a sense of calm menace. A predator pretending at disinterest.

I wince as Seamus has a close call with a white bubble, dodging under the orb at the last moment.

Then, a pop like a firecracker goes off.

"Carmichael hit a red one!" Sonya has her eyes affixed to one of the mermen.

We watch as shock gets replaced by a fierce scowl.

"Gods-damn these bubbles to the netherworld!" He howls the curse at the sky, his entire body flushing red.

"Made him angry?" Sonya speculates, and I'd have to agree.

Especially when he stalks toward a massive blue bubble and tries to throw a punch at it. This one lets out a sad fizzle as it pops. The man, Carmichael, gazes at his hand and then lets out a low moan. When he lifts his face, tears streak down his cheeks.

"Why did I do that?" Then, he buries his face in his hands and sobs.

Meanwhile, the other mythics redouble their efforts to avoid the emotional triggers as the waters grow choppy with people catching up. Someone who must not have seen the merman's breakdown dives headfirst into a green bubble, coming up a second later with a grimace.

"I think I'm going to be sick," they moan, shoving a tall redhead out of their way.

A man falls into a purple bubble. He rights himself quickly, a polite smile on his face. As a small woman approaches, the ginger shuffles to the side, clearing a path.

"After you. I insist." His polite voice disappears under the high-pitched scream of another competitor.

"What the hell?" I search out the source and find an unknown mythic flailing about despite nothing attacking them.

"Hit a white one. Fear, I'm guessing." Sonya stands taller on the branch to get a better view of the field.

I only need to see one man, and he's currently trying to get around the screecher. Unfortunately, their thrashing sends a wave carrying a yellow bubble straight into Seamus's chest.

"Oh no," I whisper before holding my breath, wondering what reaction my selkie will have.

He stumbles in the waist-high water and then slows. The sound of laughter emits from his throat. And not one quick bark. No, my selkie peals off into an unending stream of giggles.

Sonya and I exchange wide-eyed stares.

"Uh, guess that's better than screaming. Right?" My cousin doesn't sound sure.

Seamus's hilarity sounds manic, but unlike some of the people who've hit bubbles, he continues forward. Soon, the air fills with sounds of sobbing and laughter and the occasional scream. I breathe a sigh of relief when Seamus breaks away from the field of bubbles, but tension continues to thrum through my bones when the effects don't immediately wear off. He presses through the water, cackling all the while.

From my vantage point, Seamus appears to be in third place. Tanvi and Xavier are just a few yards ahead. All three aim for a cliff face. The top is the finish line. A thirty-foot climb, and this strange Gauntlet can end.

Just as I'm about to wing myself to the top, Sonya wraps her fingers around my bicep.

"Things aren't over down here."

Dread clutches at my stomach a moment before a roar shakes the leaves of the nearby trees. A cheer soars from the spectators as a furry, giant mass bursts from the tree line and hurtles into the water in front of the competitors, blocking their way to the cliff.

The salt-and-pepper shimmer of the ferocious animal's coat glistens in the midday sun in a familiar way.

"Oh my gods. Is that ..."

"Yep." Sonya grins wide. "Heath."

33

———

SEAMUS

Heath is gigantic.

Shifters in animal form always differ slightly from the true animal. They might have an interesting-colored coat or oddly shaped faces. I even met a shifter that maintained a vocal box while in their bobcat form. Creepy, talking to them, but fascinating all the same.

Heath's difference is simpler. He's huge. At least twice the size of a grizzly. I'm betting he has a few hundred pounds on a polar bear. The guy releases a ground-shaking roar that stirs up waves in the shallow water.

Despite my continued chuckling, I am not amused in the slightest.

They expect me to fight my way past him?

Even with both my arms back in commission, the task is impossible. I glance to my left and catch Xavier's gaze. The dragon keeps his face blank, but I get the sense he's as baffled by this challenge as I am.

But Tanvi doesn't seem daunted. She eyes up Heath like he's

200

a nasty bug she needs to wipe off her windshield, not a ferocious, giant creature looking to rip off a limb. Then again, she can turn into a fearsome beast herself. Just not at the moment.

"Can't let a shifter show me up," Xavier mutters, moving the same time as Tanvi.

"You turn into a big lizard with wings. Sounds like a shifter to me," she sneers.

The dragon glares at the wolf. "You owe me a finger."

Her smirk bleeds *fuck you*. "It wasn't the whole finger. Get over it." Without warning, she lunges at Heath, only to immediately stumble back, the shallow water splashing around her calves as she dodges a clawed paw the size of a trash-can lid aimed straight for her head.

I know the baker gets grumpy sometimes, but I've never seen him in bear form, ready to brawl. Still, it's not like he has many wrestling buddies. Maybe this is how he lets off steam.

"Are we sure this is a fight?" I ask no one in particular. The Winged One is known for loving tricks, and the sirens are often like their creator. "Maybe we get another riddle?"

Heath huffs a snort and then charges toward me—and not in a *I'm going to whisper a puzzle in your ear* kind of way. I dive to the side but still get slammed in the chest by a meaty shoulder. Over the splash of the water, I think I hear something crack. A dull throb starts up in my chest.

That's going to be black and blue tomorrow.

And I guess he just answered my question.

"If he wants a fight, I'll give him one." Xavier's eyes glow a bright yellow as he charges forward with a battle screech.

Heath rises onto his hind legs, and just as the dragon looks ready to sink a set of claws into the guy's furry belly, the shifter moves faster than a beast his size has the right to, scooping Xavier up in a bear hug. One meant to pulverize bones.

Suddenly, my ribs don't feel too bad.

Unfortunately, while Heath is focused on Xavier, Tanvi

takes her chance, dodging around the battling mythics and arrowing straight for the foot of the cliff.

Just when I'm sure she has the competition won, a brown blur smashes into her.

That's right. Heath has a cousin, I think to myself. Too late to share the knowledge with anyone else.

The smaller yet still very large and very intimidating bear shifter lifts Tanvi into the air and gives her a mighty toss. He throws her so far that she lands on the edge of the bubble field, smashing into a red globe. The werewolf rises from the water, fury twisting her face.

Oh no.

Laughter still spills out of me in random bursts, which means her rage isn't going to fade soon. And there's no guarantee she'll direct all that anger at the bear who threw her.

Plus, I can spy at least four more competitors almost through the bubbles. This last stretch to the finish line is going to be crowded soon, and I don't want to stick around for that total melee to begin. I need out of this. I need to use my head.

As I clutch my stomach through another round of hilarity, I turn in time to watch Heath drop Xavier into the water. The dragon groans out a string of curses. Heath's cousin swings his massive head around, focus landing on me.

I'm not a fighter. Not even in selkie form. Moira might be able to take the bear down with just her force of will but not me. I need another avenue besides charging the shifter head-on.

Maybe if I compliment his pastries, he'll let me pass.

The thought is flippant, born from desperation, but when I spy the dragon slowly straightening, I know my chance to get ahead is dwindling fast.

So, I act on the instinct.

Stepping into Heath's eyeline, I try to project my voice, even as whatever he did to my ribs makes pulling in a full breath difficult.

"Your croissants"—I giggle—"are flaky"—a painful gasp —"and delicious!" I shout at the growling beast and cringe through the resulting ache.

Heath fixes two ice-blue eyes on me, and the dragon gives me a strange look right along with him.

"What?" I raise my arms in a helpless, painful shrug. "I'm not lying."

Then, much to my shock, Heath steps to the side. Clearing a path for me.

Unless this is a trick, that actually worked. Even as I want to stand there and marvel at my absurd genius, I catch a glimpse of Neri high up in a tree. Watching me.

No room for hesitation. I don't want her to think I'm second-guessing any part of this competition. Plus, Xavier is going to get over his pissy attitude any second and find a way to compliment the bear that just tried to crush his lungs.

"Thanks." I laugh the word and try not to wince as I half-waddle, half-run past the shifter. My body stays braced for a sneak attack up until I press my palms against the sun-warmed stone of the cliff.

Thirty feet. Straight up. Don't give up. Show her I know how to fight for things—even if I can't hold my own against a thousand-pound bear.

As I fit my fingers and toes into uneven notches, I try not to breathe too deep. Mythics might heal faster than humans but not enough to knit a rib back in place in minutes. I would need a healing witch for that. Maybe I can find one when this is all over and pay whatever exorbitant price they demand.

For now, I do my best to ignore the pain and pull myself higher.

There's a wheeze below me, and I make the mistake of looking down. Just ten feet below, the dragon has dug his sharp claws into the cliff face, getting a better hold than I could ever hope for. No doubt he'll overtake me in seconds.

Damn The Finned One's games.

I guess I didn't realize how much I wanted to win this thing. How desperate I am to. Yeah, maybe Neri will appreciate the effort I've put in so far, but I have this fear lingering in my gut that even this won't be enough.

So, I need it all, just in case.

But the dragon is going to steal the win from me in the last moment.

At least, he would if there wasn't an infuriated werewolf clinging to his leg.

And when I say werewolf, I mean, fully changed. Maybe the rage bubble was too much for Tanvi. For whatever reason, she's disqualified herself with the transformation. Not that being out of the race has calmed her down at all. Tanvi is fearsome in her other form. Snarling and growling as she sinks massive fangs into Xavier's thigh.

"Let go, Tanvi! Gods-damn it, I don't want to hurt you!" The dragon shakes his leg, as if that might dislodge her, and I spare a thought for how odd it is to hear Xavier more concerned for the wolf's safety than his own.

"I got this!" The call comes from a siren, the woman swooping toward us with her red-tipped wings glistening in the sun.

When I spy a green cloth ball in her gloved hand, I can guess what'll happen next. Not waiting around for my lead to disappear, I put my last reserves of energy into heaving myself the rest of the way up the sheer rock wall. My fingers finally curve around the top ledge, and I could cry in relief when I roll my body over the edge onto solid ground.

I've never been so happy to get out of the water.

34

______

NERI

THE MOMENT SEAMUS collapses on the top of the cliff, I dive
down to him, folding my wings close to my body, only to unfurl
them at the last moment to soften my landing. The edge he
mounted was the finish line, which means I can touch him
without interfering with the Gauntlet.

He won.

A prick of shame heats my neck when I realize at no point
did I think he'd make it all the way to the end. Much less before
everyone else.

Turns out, I underestimated my bookish professor.

"Are you hurt?" The beginnings of a beard scrape my palms
as I gently cup his face. "Seamus? Are you okay?"

Soft brown eyes blink up at me. Then, a cascade of chuckles
bursts from his throat. "You—you make everything better." He
laughs some more, but the look in his eyes isn't humorous.

I might call it worshipful.

Those fluttering sensations dip and dive through my chest,
but I stifle them with practicality.

"That's sweet, but my presence doesn't magically fix internal bleeding." As far as I can see, he hasn't sustained any surface wounds. Still. "I saw you get shoulder-checked by Heath. You're going to be a bruised mess tomorrow." Carefully, I run my hands down his neck, over his shoulders, along his chest.

"Really? Here?" The selkie raises his eyebrows. "Well, I'm not usually an exhibitionist, but for you—"

"Shut up," I murmur the chastisement without heat.

My fingers reach his ribs, and Seamus gasps in pain and then lets out a string of giggles. Whoever the witch is that created those bubbles, she must be strong for the effects to still linger like this.

"I think you have a broken rib. Or at least a cracked one. We need to get you to a doctor. Or a witch."

"Wait." Seamus grasps my hand as I move to stand. "Not yet."

That's when I realize he and I aren't alone on this cliff top. A few more competitors have summited the climb, lying not too far away, panting out their own exhaustion. Spectators have taken the easier paths that loop through the forest on either side of the cliff to reach the top.

Then, there are the sirens. Dozens of my kind descending from above, glorious with their imposing wings tipped in crimson. They form a half-circle around us. From the gathering, Zelda steps forward, cradling an intricately carved figurine. The figure has been crafted from solid mahogany, her form dressed only in the pattern of the wood grain. From her back sprouts a set of wings, the tips jagged, as they end too soon.

Galen.

"As head of Galen's Gauntlet committee, it is my honor to present this—"

"Wait!" The shout comes in a familiar haughty voice, even more painful to my eardrums than the shrieks emitted by the competitors who came into contact with a white bubble.

A muscle tics in Zelda's jaw, but that's the only crack in the siren's calm exterior. "Pamela. Is there a reason you're interrupting this moment honoring Galen?"

The siren in question steps out of the group, shooting a glare at the committee head. "Yes, there is. You were about to announce the wrong winner. Seamus MacNamara *remembered* my song. The competition was unfair. He should be disqualified." Pamela lifts her chin, righteousness seeping off her in waves.

The crowd grumbles and mutters, but I can't make out if they are for or against her.

Doesn't matter because I know where I stand.

"Are you fucking kidding me?" I lunge to my feet, wings splayed wide with my fury, ready to do damage. "Seamus went through everything else that the others did. He just scaled a cliff with a broken rib! How is that unfair?"

The older siren gives a disapproving sniff as a response. Zelda's calm countenance melts into an evil grin that I might shiver under the attention of if it were aimed at me.

"Interesting." Zelda turns her focus fully on Pamela, not letting the woman squirm away even if she wanted to. "Do you know what the rules of the Gauntlet state? Because I do. Section B, paragraph two: *No sirens, whether residents of Folk Haven or of foreign location, are allowed to take part in the Gauntlet as a competitor.*"

"We're not talking about a siren." Pamela tries to hold her high ground, but her confidence cracks under Zelda's powerful presence.

"Section B, paragraph five," the committee head continues as if the other woman never spoke, "*Competitors in the Gauntlet must be of mythic origin. No humans may take part even if they are mated to a mythic partner.*"

"We are not discussing a human," Pamela grinds out the words through a stiff jaw.

"Amendment five, made in the year 1983: *No witches may take part as competitors but are free to offer their services as developers of the Gauntlet.*"

"Again," Pamela growls, "we are discuss—"

"Those," Zelda says over her, "are all the rules that stipulate the nature of those who may enter Galen's Gauntlet. Do you know why that is?"

Pamela's wings quiver in what I guess is suppressed rage. For those who thought the day's entertainment was done, they must not have realized a post-Gauntlet verbal sparring match would take place.

"I'll tell you," Zelda says when the siren remains silent. "Because adding a rule stating *no siren mates*, also known as the beings who can recall what sirens have sung, would be admitting that a siren could possibly enter into a relationship with someone *other* than a fellow siren or human. Now, why do you think the original writers of these rules had a problem with that?"

"Because cross-mythic mating is wrong," Pamela hisses with so much venom that I wonder if my kind might have a poison-spewing ability I wasn't aware of.

"Odd." The word comes in a husky, confident voice, and I glance to the side, finding that Moira has found her way out of the love cage and joined the group. "That you would hold such a prejudice against a siren-selkie relationship when the woman this competition celebrates fell in love with a selkie herself."

Good point.

Crouching down, I offer Seamus my arm to help him rise to his feet, taking as much of his weight as he's willing to give. In this moment, I realize how utterly right I feel beside him. As if spanning the decades, I've found a connection to my ancestor. A woman who loved a man Of the Fin.

I wonder if Galen found her selkie lover as frustratingly irresistible as I do mine.

"Galen might have strayed from the proper path during hard times." Pamela maintains her prim air of disdain, even as her face flushes darker than the paint on her wings. "But I am sure once she defeated the sorcerer, she did the right thing."

"You mean, she got far away from ungrateful bigots and banged her selkie lover's brains out?" Sonya asks loud enough for all those gathered to hear.

A riotous cheer goes up through the crowd, filling my heart with hope that Pamela's kind are just a small, dark blip in an otherwise accepting town. But with a twist of my heart, I realize that I don't know Galen's selkie's name. The song leaves him unidentified, as if he wasn't important enough to remember.

Goes to show, the history keepers affect what we're allowed to remember.

Once the whooping and laughter quiet down, Zelda holds up the Galen figurine to regain everyone's attention.

"You may be surprised to hear, Pamela, but I'm inclined to agree with you."

My throat tightens, and if I wasn't supporting Seamus, I'd step forward, ready to battle for him.

But the siren isn't done.

"Gaining the love of a siren could potentially give someone an advantage." Zelda dips her chin at the smug smile curling over Pamela's mouth. "However, seems to me, every competitor had the same chance to try their hand at wooing one of our kind."

Pamela's expression turns sour quick.

"It is no mystery that siren song is used during the Gauntlet. And this might be an issue the committee should address. In the future. As of now, there's no rule barring a mythic simply because a siren loves them. The original ruling stands. Seamus MacNamara is the winner of this year's Gauntlet."

A roar of cheers shakes the treetops, and I'm relieved to see that there isn't a consensus to spurn Seamus's win. He earned it, as far as I'm concerned.

As Zelda rattles off the list of prizes that go along with winning, I focus on the selkie sagging into my side. I make sure to keep my hold at his hip rather than his chest to avoid pressing on his rib. I just want all of this over with, so he can receive medical help.

"And now"—Zelda's voice takes on a ringing quality, regaining my attention—"we honor the siren who suffered so that we might live free."

All together, the sirens raise their voices, singing the final three verses of the song that tells Galen's story.

He tried to rule us
To collect us
He said he was the darkness
But the night is where we thrive

He's the beginning
Not the ending
Galen he could not possess
She's the reason we survive

So, swim deep
And fly high
Dig your claws into the earth
Claim your freedom and your pride

Most here won't remember the song in the next second, but

when I stare up at Seamus's face, I watch awe settle over his features. He'll remember.

"Seamus MacNamara, you honored Galen's name today."

Zelda steps forward and offers the wooden statue to him. He accepts, his jaw tightening as he grits his teeth through the movement.

"I am honored. The competition was fierce."

My selkie nods toward the others he raced against, and they dip their chins in returned respect.

"The final reward you receive comes from the sirens. You may request knowledge that we hold in our sacred songs, or you may ask a favor of any of us. Now or at any point in the future."

From the corner of my eye, I watch a twist of disgust overtake Pamela's mouth, as if she thinks he's going to demand that she scrub his toilet for the next year.

Not a bad idea. Maybe I should suggest it.

"I'll ask now."

My body tightens at his words, and a spike of panic goes through my chest.

He wouldn't use his favor on me, would he? Requesting that I be his mate in order to fulfill the requirements of the Gauntlet?

Immediately, I reject the thought.

Seamus would not force me. He knows the importance of free choice.

"Ask then," Zelda intones.

A hush falls over the crowd.

Seamus stands taller, keeping his arm around my shoulders but taking on all of his own weight. He turns enough to gaze into my eyes. Brown against gray, we hold each other.

"I would like wisdom. I would like to know how I might make Neri Onassis happy for the rest of her life."

My body shudders as too many emotions crash within me.

Some people in the gathering laugh; others coo.

There's a loud scoff before I hear Moira's deep voice. "Gods-damn it, Seamus! Ask something useful next time, why don't you?"

My selkie grins wide but doesn't take his stare from me. "So, what's the answer?"

Needing privacy in this world-altering moment, I encircle us in my wings, creating a curtain between us and the rest of the world. Standing on my toes, I bring my mouth to his ear.

"You." I press a quick kiss against his jaw. "And books, of course."

35

NERI

THE MEASURING tape lets out a definitive slap as I let it recoil. The sound echoes through the empty shop.

Empty for now.

Already, I have visions in my mind of where bookshelves will stand with comfortable seats at their ends. My imagination strings lights from the ceiling and covers the hardwood floor in thick area rugs.

I try to rein myself in, not wanting to mentally spend a whole bank account of money I don't have. Silently, I pray to The Winged One my application for a small business loan from the sirens' fund is accepted. Luckily, Pamela is not on the deciding board, so I think I might have a chance.

If not, I'll figure something out. Too much hope courses through my veins to ever contemplate giving up on this dream.

My own bookshop. Tingles skitter over my skin at the idea.

But even this joy can't fully distract from the empty space looming in my life for the last few days.

One shaped exactly like Seamus MacNamara.

I haven't seen the selkie since we left Folk Haven's emergency care center. Seamus refused to pay the exorbitant price a healing witch would charge for an injury he claimed would heal in a matter of days. The stubborn mythic settled for a nurse wrapping his ribs up.

Then, the most ridiculous words came from his mouth.

"I need time to utilize the knowledge you gave me. I won't be around for a short while."

I went full dying fish on him, mouth bobbing open with an utter lack of words.

"You're beautiful," he said, dropping a kiss on my forehead before gingerly hobbling toward a parked car.

Owen sat behind the wheel and gave me a wave.

I ignored him.

"Did Heath knock out your brain too?" I shouted after Seamus's retreating form, not caring that we stood on Main Street. "I told you, I need you!"

"I need you too," he called back and then waved over his shoulder. "See you in a few days."

If he wasn't already injured, I might have stabbed him.

After I had time to curse him to all the gods, I reasoned with myself that this distance would be a good thing. Make sure I wasn't swept up in the grand-gesture moment. Took me about an hour to get over that bullshit thought, and I went right back to being pissy.

Now, I'm just lonely. Even surrounded by people all day at Coffee & Claws and then engulfed at night by sirens who come over for perpetual happy hour at Sonya's house.

But there's a difference between being alone and being lonely.

Two days ago, I broke down and drove over to his house, ready to tip a few tables over if I discovered him leisurely reading in his library. Instead, I found the lights off, house empty. However, there was a number code lock on the front door, and above the keypad, there was a note.

Neri,

Type in the day you flew.

My heart swelled. He hadn't forgotten me.

Thinking back to the date of when I'd first unfurled my wings in his library, I plugged in the numbers. When the lock clicked open, little bubbles of joy arose in my chest.

Much more pleasant than the bubbles of mystery emotions from the Gauntlet.

Just as it seemed from the outside, Seamus's house was empty. But he clearly meant to give me full access. I turned on lights, found a book, and snuggled into a cushy armchair that smelled like warm clay and the man I loved. For that evening, I was mollified.

Now, I'm back to pouting.

"Hey, babe." Sonya enters through the doorway that leads to the back of the shop. "How's it going?"

Since she's asking about the business and not my love life, I'm able to answer on a positive note.

"Good so far. We have plenty of room for the shelving even if we want to add a seating area by the window. I'm still debating if I want the counter in the back or the front. I think I'll bring some painters tape over and map things out on the floor. Get a better idea of the arrangement."

"Sounds like you're chugging along." My cousin squeezes my shoulder; that simple gesture conveys more support than I've received from my parents.

With a clear idea of my path forward, I decided to reach out to them. Give them an update on my life, so they wouldn't have to worry.

Guess being away from them for a few months had me forgetting that worry was what they did best.

"Oh no. No, honey. Bookshops aren't a good investment. You know everyone uses electronic readers these days. And in a small town? Those are dying, honey. You need to move back here. If you don't like the idea of running the restaurant, we can figure something else out. And you know, we just talked to the Lancasters ..."

As my mom continued talking about my ex, the safe human picked out for me, I accepted that my move hadn't spurred them to reconsider their treatment of me. I had gone across the country to get away, and they still wanted to draw me back into their cocoon.

But I refused to go.

"I'm in love with Seamus MacNamara," I said loud enough to drown out my mother's description of Ronald's new car. "He's not perfect, but he's right for me. I sing around him. And I stretch my wings when we're together—" I paused for just a moment at my mother's gasp, but then I pressed on. "And he's a selkie! We're mates. But even if we weren't, I'd never go back to Ronald, and I'm never going back to where I have to pretend I'm human for the rest of my life." I was panting, high on the energy of telling my truth. "When you and Dad can accept that, I'd love for you to come to Folk Haven for a visit. Until then, we need more time apart."

"Neri! How could—"

"Good-bye, Mom." And I hung up.

After two days of furious, pleading voice mails and text messages from both my parents, I sent them a message, reminding them they knew where to find me when their minds changed.

Then, I blocked their numbers.

Strange how an action can break a heart while also liberating it.

"I have the key to your new place. Thought you'd want to check out upstairs too. Maybe start moving your stuff in. Not that I'm trying to get rid of you."

Sonya slings an arm around my shoulders, leading me toward the back of the building. We exit through one door, only to turn to one immediately beside it.

"Last tenant left a few things. Figure it's up for grabs." Sonya holds out a keychain with two shiny silver keys. "Just installed new locks."

"You think I'm going to have some trouble?" I joke.

Sonya's mouth twists. "Not of the breaking-and-entering sort. Not really Pamela's style."

I stiffen at the name of the siren who loves shooting dagger glares my way whenever we cross paths around town. "You really think she hates inter-mythic relationships enough to hold a grudge?"

A weighted pause descends, heavy as the evening's humidity. Sonya grips my shoulders, staring deep into my eyes. "I would love to tell you that Folk Haven is a mythic paradise, where we never have to worry about living our lives the way we want. But I can't say that. Humans aren't the only ones who hate people just for being different."

When the siren speaks next, her words ring with a power my heart wants to call prophecy. "But things are changing. I can feel it in my bones as much as I see it with my eyes. Some of our kind think just because their grandparents made this town, this lake, that they have the right to dictate how things will be. But Folk Haven is young. Ripe for growth. You spend decades gathering mythics into one location; you'd have to be naive to think we'd all follow some rigid rules dictated from a place of fear."

"I don't care what anyone says. If Seamus and I want to be together, we will be." The conviction in my voice flows through my body in a surge of power, and Sonya offers me a smile that has a twinge of sadness.

"One day, I expect your relationship will be normal among our kind. I'm sorry that you have to be among the first. That you'll have to fight more hate than most."

My mind brings up the map in Moira's office, trailing to the far corner, where the monsters of Lake Galen have their homes. The offspring of a love like mine. Of a love like Galen's.

"We're not the first." I cover her hands with mine, squeezing tight. "I think I just thought of a name for the bookshop."

"Oh yeah? What's that?"

"Never Judge a Cover."

Sonya laughs, a small chuckle at first that grows into a full-blown belly laugh. "I'm so glad you moved to town, little cousin." She swipes tears from her eyes and plants a kiss on my cheek. "Let me know if you don't want anything inside. I'm happy to toss it in the dumpster for you." My cousin says the last bit with a gleeful twinkle, as if she enjoys putting things in the garbage.

Maybe I should have her help me purge my overwhelming book collection.

Ha. Not likely.

"Will do."

I slide the key into the lock of my new home. *Mine.*

Well, mine as much as renting a place is. But one day, I'll own all this outright. I know I will. Not because I think it's fated. But because I know what I want now and I'm going after it with everything I have.

The stairs let out a welcoming creak as I climb to the second floor, encountering another door. After unlocking this one, too, I step into an open space.

The apartment is empty, except for a few piles of books and a selkie.

My selkie.

"Neri." Seamus speaks my name through a grin and then schools his features to be serious. "I want to thank you for giving me time to absorb the wisdom you provided. I expect you'll be happy with the research I've pursued these last few days."

"I would've been happier with you, you infuriating selkie!" I growl the words.

Seamus nods, trying to suppress a smile and failing horribly. "Really?"

"Winged One"—I raise my arms to the ceiling in supplication—"deliver me from dense men."

"Sorry, sorry." Seamus makes a placating gesture. "I'll get to the point. I've been in Atlanta."

"Why?" Exasperation shoves the word from my throat.

Seamus gestures to the piles of books around him. "I went to their bookstores."

Shifting forward, I get a better look at the covers of the novels he gathered. I only need a moment to scan their cracked spines to realize the connection.

"They're romance novels."

"Yes. Exactly. Also, I am embarrassingly ignorant. Or at least, I hope I can say I *was* ignorant and am now at least nearing the end of beginner-level knowledge of the genre, soon to achieve intermediate status. But that is likely hopeful thinking, as I've only been reading for five days. However, I am quite a fast reader and have consumed ten novels of varying subgenres of romance while I've been away."

"Seamus, you're getting muddled." My lips threaten to curl despite my vexation. "What are you trying to say?"

"Ah, yes. The point I am trying to make is that I don't simply want to give you books to make you happy. Although I certainly will, no doubt to bribe you into forgiving me for future lapses I'm bound to make—"

"Seamus."

"Yes. Right. The point. The point is, I want our literature to overlap and intwine, creating a clear model for our love to follow. I don't want to simply give you things and hope they make you happy. I want to experience them with you. Read with you. Live life with you."

He scoops up a book off the top of one pile. "I went to all the independent bookstores in Atlanta and found the ones that have romance sections. I made a list." His fingers slip into a pocket and pull out a piece of paper. "That way, you won't have to be disappointed when we go back there together by showing up to a shop and realizing they don't stock romance titles. Also, I asked the booksellers for their recommendations and came away with all of these." He gestures to the small collection at his feet. "As you know, my home library is sorely lacking in romance, so this is just a start. As I mentioned, I began reading them, and that's when I realized how truly ignorant I was."

Seamus meets my eyes, his blazing with the fire of a new book convert. "These stories are amazing. You had every right to shove me in the lake for calling them fluff. I deserve worse."

I press my knuckles against my lips as emotions overwhelm me, threatening to emit some strange noises from my throat. All the while, Seamus continues waxing poetic about romance.

"The emotional depth is staggering. And the emphasis on developing healthy relationships—not to mention, the focus on female pleasure. Of course, the patriarchy scorns romance. I am embarrassed at my density. And besides all that, there is the intricate world-building. Like in this one"—he holds up a novel with a pale, dark-haired woman wearing a magenta ballgown —"I learned about smugglers in nineteenth-century Britain using ice boats to hide illegal goods. And here"—Seamus snags a book with a Black couple embracing—"this takes readers through the struggles of former slaves in Louisiana, post–Civil War. And still, the characters build a loving relationship. And the author cited her sources! Have you read this one?" Seamus extends the romance novel to me. "I'd love to discuss it with you."

My ability to speak disappears. This is too much.

The man I love scoured bookstores for romance novels for me. He admitted he was wrong without trying to excuse himself. He then read the romance novels and now wants to discuss them.

Is there anything hotter in the world?

"Also, I came across a costume shop while I was in Atlanta. Does role-play interest you? I wouldn't mind acting out a few of the scenes."

I think my vagina just combusted.

Unable to hold back any longer, I launch myself across the room, straight into Seamus's waiting arms. Before he can say another word that will turn my brain to mush, I claim his mouth.

I claim him.

"You are"—I kiss him hard—"the most"—a kiss to the corner of his mouth—"infuriating"—I press my lips to the other corner—"amazing"—lick his bottom lip—"man."

Seamus wraps his arms tight around me as my onslaught continues, holding me against his chest. When we finally break apart, panting and flushed, his curious gaze meets mine.

"Is that a yes to the romance-hero role-play?"

A shiver works through my body, and there's a tingle at my shoulder blades. My wings want out, and I want my mate inside me.

"You're the only hero I want." I cup his face, tracing my thumbs along his cheekbones. "But maybe also a cowboy."

36

———

NERI

I ALMOST HAVE the bookshelves exactly right when the front bell rings, announcing an arrival to my as-yet unfinished bookshop.

"I don't need a massage, is all I'm saying. I'm perfectly relaxed!" Moira's familiar voice echoes around the space that isn't as empty as it was last week.

"Relaxed people tend not to shout in public places," my selkie replies to his sister, even as he grins at me. "Wouldn't you agree, Neri?"

"Shouting is how I get rid of my stress." Moira glares at her brother and then turns her stare to me. "Tell him. A good shout or two is better than some stranger touching all over your body."

"Well, when you put it that way ..." I hedge, fighting against a smile at their bickering.

"Wait, no." Seamus waves his hands to halt my response. "She says *stranger* like a random person on the street. We're talking about a highly trained professional at a luxury spa.

People pay hundreds for their skills."

"I don't see a difference." Moira thrusts her chin into the air and makes like she's browsing the stack of used paperbacks I weeded from my own collection and plan to sell in the shop.

Now that I finally have a place to unpack all my belongings as well as an entire bookstore full of titles in my future, I found the strength to get rid of some less sentimental items in my personal library.

"Are we talking about Haven's Relaxation?"

Everyone in Folk Haven knows about the new business venture. There are mixed feelings about a place likely to put our town on more tourists' radars, but nothing has stopped the spa from moving ahead.

"Yes. My sister here gets to sample the services before anyone else, and she's complaining about it," Seamus explains, shaking his head in overexaggerated disappointment.

"I'm not a spa person," she throws over her shoulder. "Don't see what the appeal is."

"I'm looking forward to the opening," I admit. Despite her growly behavior, I know Moira appreciates honesty over placation. "Levi agreed to set up a satellite bookstore in the lobby." I finally learned the name of my *flavored coffee with oat milk and cocoa powder* customer. Levi Abadi, the monster representative on Folk Haven's council and fellow new business owner. "Just a small shelf with a selection of the latest best sellers. A lot of people find reading relaxing. I thought they might be inclined to purchase something to read during their stay."

"I love your bookish business mind," Seamus murmurs as he leans his elbows on my brand-new counter and gazes at me like I'm made of chocolate cake.

"Get a room," Moira mutters. "I'll take this one." She holds up a paperback. "How much?"

"A dollar."

She drops the book in her purse, fishes out a dollar, and slaps the bill on the counter.

My first sale! I'll have to frame this one.

Even though I didn't get a clear view of the book cover, I'm pretty sure I recognized the spine. The selkie grabbed herself a steamy romance. One with a hero that shares some uncanny similarities to a certain dark-haired monster. The one Moira got locked in a love cage with and was rumored to have accompanied her on an overnight road trip not too long ago.

"Enjoy." I keep my voice and smile at a customer-service-level brightness. I don't see any reason to judge a woman for her reading habits, even as interesting as I think they are.

Moira leaves with a wave to me and a middle finger to her brother.

"Ah, sibling love. So pure." I grin at my selkie, and he smirks back.

"Don't worry. One day, she'll be flipping you off too."

"Can't wait." Surprisingly, I'm telling the truth. I love the idea of being so ingrained in the MacNamara clan that I could get into a shouting match with them and still have their love when it was all over.

Seamus wanders around as I straighten up enough to keep the area safe, and then he walks with me upstairs. Despite our recent matehood declaration—which was all that was required to make things official—I told him I wanted to live in the apartment above the bookshop, at least for a little while.

And proving just how great a partner he was working on becoming, Seamus didn't push back. Didn't argue that he had a house I loved and I should be eager to move in with him.

All he asked was if he could stay with me. While I wanted a place that was mine, I didn't want to sleep without him ever again. We came up with a plan. Weekdays, we'd stay in the bookshop apartment because it shortened both of our commutes. But on weekends, we'd go back to the lake house, spending the evenings lounging in our dream library.

Perfection.

At least, it will be as long as The Council doesn't push back on a siren spending so much time in Of the Fin territory. Apparently, the ruling body meets the first Monday of every month, which is just over a week away. The decision about the witch library will happen, and my bet is that the choice could set Folk Haven on a different path. One where I can live wherever I want with my selkie mate.

I hope The Council members choose to look forward rather than stay in the past.

Tonight, Seamus is in charge of dinner, and as I watch him slide a dish into the oven, I can't help thinking back on the day in his kitchen when everything almost went up in flames.

The memory has me smiling.

"So, I have a theory," I announce, rising from the couch Seamus's parents gave me as a housewarming present.

"Ah." He slips the oven mitts off as he shoots me a grin. "You know I love theories. Please do go on."

"I theorize that the selkie mate lore was created in response to the fact that selkies are notoriously clumsy and the people who love them just happen to be the ones nearby, willing to jump in and save them. So, it's not that we're *fated* to be together. You just awkwardly stumbled your way into trouble, and I dived in to help because I was a decent person and I couldn't let such a sexy professor die on my watch." As I meander up behind him, I catch a glimpse of a smirk.

"This theory holds merit. You might have enough for a thesis."

"Should I try earning my doctorate in seducing selkies?"

Seamus whirls around, and finding me so close, he scoops me up and carries me down the short hall to where we sleep.

"Not sure I want you researching anywhere outside of our bedroom."

I yelp when he tosses me onto the mattress and then try to affect a casual tone. "Hmm. Not even in the library?" I bite my lips as I stare up at him, loving how his curls fall haphazardly over his forehead. "Or on the dock?" My knees fall apart, a clear invitation. "Or the restroom at Local Brew?"

"That was one time, and you had just agreed to be my mate and then plied me with all those fruity drinks!" Seamus launches himself on top of me as I giggle evilly. "Now, we know rum makes me horny," he mutters against my hair, rocking his stiff erection between my legs, eliciting a gasp.

"I guess this means, you've been drinking rum today?" Wrapping a leg around his waist, I pull Seamus snug against me.

He groans deep in his throat. "Drunk on you," he mutters.

Just as I'm about to bite the lobe of his ear, my selkie mate pulls his head back, soft brown eyes gazing down at me.

"I have a theory."

I groan and sling my other leg around his waist. "Tell me once you're inside me."

Seamus's lids flutter, but he shakes his head slow, our noses brushing. "My theory is that my ancestors might have been clumsy, but they were also smart." The intensity of his voice pricks at my nipples. "They knew if someone saved them, that person was worth knowing. Someone whose love they might be lucky to have."

A vulnerability seeps into my chest. "But that doesn't always hold true." Thoughts of Ginger threaten my happiness.

Seamus holds my stare. "The saving tells us to take notice. The loving comes from knowing. I know you, Neri. More every day. And I only fall deeper in love with you."

The brief doubt floats away. "You keep falling." I press a gentle kiss to the point of his nose. "I'll catch you."

EPILOGUE

LEVI

In a far corner of Lake Galen ...

THE HUMID NIGHT air sneaks in between my clothes and my skin, sticking them together in an uncomfortable marriage as I approach the gaudiest house on Lake Galen. The place stands three stories tall, the roof almost as high as the peaks of the pine trees. Glossy stone columns frame the double-door entrance, the pillars jutting high enough to support the massive roof and giving the sense of entering a palace rather than a home. The front porch is made entirely of marble.

Can it even be called a porch?

More like a giant pedestal.

The glass of the windows sits in panes of gold that glitter in the dying light of the day. Through the clear portals, I spy a hint of plush velvet drapery hanging just inside.

How has this monstrosity not slid into the lake yet?

One heavy rain, and the thing could be riding a mudslide to a watery grave.

Even with all this opulence, one of the oddest details is the set of massive hyena statues that sit like sentries on either side of the doorway. The beasts were carved from black marble, the dark color adding extra menace to their grinning mouths full of jagged fangs.

A loud crash sounds from inside the abode, and I push aside my reluctance to enter this house of curiosities without an escort. The front doors open easily, silent on well-oiled hinges.

"Sev?" I call out the owner's name as I step into a foyer that would make European royalty proud. "I got your message. Are you all right?"

There's an inarticulate shout and another crash.

"I'm coming in!" *Please don't kill me*, I pray silently.

Jogging toward the sound of struggling, I enter a grand dining room and find the owner of the house.

Sev wears his human form, that of a lean-muscled white man with golden hair cascading past his shoulders. Most of the world would call him devastatingly attractive. But that doesn't change the fact that to all mythics, Sev—like me—is a monster.

And he's currently naked, grappling with a creature from nightmares.

The thing resembles a skeleton brought to life, only sharper, covered in a milk-white flesh and possessing a skull similar to that of a fish. One from deep in the ocean with needle teeth and sightless eyes.

"Oh, good. You've arrived." The nude man somehow maintains a casual tone, even as the bony creature thrashes in his grip. "I've found your thief. No need to thank me. Not at the moment anyway. However, I might ask that you assist in the restraining. For not having muscle, the bastard is surprisingly strong."

Sev might as well be talking about the weather; he seems so unaffected. But I can spot the strain in his tight jaw.

Cursing, I circle the table fast and grab hold of one flailing limb and then another. Then, somehow, I find myself as the only one with a grip on the creature as Sev strolls away.

"Where are you going?" I shout while avoiding snapping teeth.

"To get a solution." The monster disappears through a doorway.

As I wait for him to return, hoping he hasn't abandoned me, I try to study the struggling thing in my hold. The creature doesn't make it easy.

"I won't hurt you." I attempt a soothing voice. "I'm a monster too." Because that must be what this is. Another odd combination of mythic genetics. "Do you have a human form?" Not all monsters do. My next question cuts off on a gasp when a sharp limb jabs into my shin.

Sev reappears, dressed in a luxurious red robe that gapes open, showing his chest. At least he tied it at the waist to hide his swinging dick from view.

"Hold it."

"I am!"

If I wasn't, I'd punch Sev in the gut for his bored tone. Doesn't he see the spindly claws groping for my eyes?

"Here we are." With a flourish, the blond pulls out a carved figurine from a deep pocket.

The item is barely longer than a finger, and he holds the piece up for me to see. As if we were at a farmers market, discussing tomatoes instead of struggling to subdue a skeletal creature.

"Do you know how many sunken ships I had to search through to find this? You need to be extremely careful in those situations. The current, you see, can pull away anything you find if you don't keep a proper hold."

"I don't need a treasure-hunting lesson." I grunt as the creature hits my solar plexus with a particularly pointy elbow. "Just use whatever your toy is to calm this guy down."

The monster has the audacity to roll his eyes, but then he lunges forward, pressing the carving against the papery skin of the creature, and whispers a word I don't recognize. The syllables rattle through my chest, as if Sev slapped me with his voice. I'm not the only one affected. For one, the monster sags after speaking, as if the word drained him of energy.

The mysterious creature abruptly gives up its fight.

Then gives up its form.

I find my arms empty as a showering clatter sounds around me.

"What happened?" With wild eyes, I search the room, sure the creature slipped my hold. But there's no sign of any other living being.

Sev holds up the carving with a wry grin. "I commanded the creepy-crawly to take its true form." His thumb buffs the object, and I recognize the shape as a bird. Maybe a crane. "It would seem that our failed thief was nothing more than fish bones."

That's what caused the clatter. Hundreds of sharp, delicate bones falling to the tabletop and floor.

"What in all the gods' plans?" I mutter, sifting my fingers through the inanimate objects as if I might find an answer underneath the collection.

"A spell." Sev plucks up a bone and sniffs it. "The Council was wrong to point fingers our way. This is not the work of monsters. Could be a witch. More likely a sorcerer." He sounds only mildly interested, as if the mention of mythics' enemy number one isn't a concern. "I found the thief near the grave."

"The grave?" I ask with a silent hope the monster means some other significant burial site than the one that came to my mind.

"*His* grave. *Le Collectionneur*." Sev pronounces the title in a perfect French accent. "Never met the piece of scum. I was deep in the Amazon when he built his little zoo." The monster picks up a larger bone and licks it.

I try not to gag at the sight. "What are you doing?"

"Sorcerer's spells taste like copper," he explains, twisted lips thoughtful. "I detect a note. It's faint. Could be because it was an old creation, made by him, only recently awakened. Or,"—Sev gestures with the carved talisman, the crimson sleeve of his robe billowing with the grand wave—"this erased most traces of the spell."

I collapse in an ornate chair, running my fingers through my hair and trying not to pull the strands out by the roots. This is another layer of stress I do not need right now.

"What is that anyway?" I ask with a sigh, accepting that Sev might have found the bone creature but likely knows as little about it as I do. The monster simply likes to guess about things.

"A tool of The Winged One. Legend states they crafted this for a particularly talented musician one thousand years ago." The monster talks in a dreamy voice, as if he were living within the object's story. "She played her music for everyone who asked, and yet powerful men sought more. To claim her. One commanded his guards kidnap her. He locked her in a room in his palace, only letting her out to play for him and his court."

A terrifying grin stretches over Sev's face, and I try to remind myself the monster has never harmed anyone within the Folk Haven town limits. As far as I know.

"But there were two other beings who loved the woman. Both more powerful than a rich fool. One was a dragon. A blacksmith in the village where the songstress lived. The couple planned to marry before she was stolen." Sev's eyes spark, a poison-green shimmer, and I wonder if he has some dragon in his lineage.

"You know as well as I, stealing from a dragon is folly. He

went after her. When he discovered her prison, spied the thick stone walls and hundreds of guards, he knew there was a single choice. The lover took on his beast form."

Drawn into the story despite my still-racing heart, I wince in sympathy for the mythic. Dragons are powerful beasts in their scaled forms, but they don't have the easy shifting ability of other mythics. A dragon who changes must remain in their reptilian form for decades. By the time the man in the story would be able to resume his human shape, his love would have lived a long stretch of her life without him.

"He tore through the walls until he found his love, spirited her away, and burned the selfish thief to the bone on his way out. They were free. But he was trapped. As a beast, humans would hunt him, and his love would never be safe."

"So, he left her?" Suddenly, I don't want to hear the rest of the story and just want my simple question answered. "What does the talisman do?"

"Recall I said, *two* powerful beings loved the musician. Her music pierced the veil of worlds, the notes too beautiful for one plane of existence. She caught the ear of The Winged One. And when the god heard her sobs, they came to her and offered a gift."

Sev fingers the bird statue, and I go still.

Could it be true? Could the monster have a god-touched gift?

"The Winged One told the songstress to press the gift to the scaly hide of her love, speak the word *truth*, and if the mythic was more man than beast, he would return to her. She did so and soon found herself in the arms of her love. Ever since, the possessor of this artifact may command the true form of others. If they are strong enough, of course. For she had a great strength in her." The monster's mouth softens as his glittering stare traces over the powerful object.

Then, with a sleight of hand, the crane disappears, and his heavy attention lands on me.

"Why did you tell me the story?" I find myself tensing under his scrutiny, as if the man might attack. Normally, my confidence does not waver, no matter my adversary. But there is a wild thrum that seems to vibrate beneath this monster's skin that puts me on edge.

I fully believe he could kill me before I saw his lethal strike.

Sev cocks his head, as if not understanding the question. Then, he blinks the glow from his eyes and shrugs. "It's a good story. I thought you might enjoy it."

"Would've thought you preferred tragedies," I mutter.

The monster whips out a sharp laugh. "I've lived over two hundred years on this hellscape humans have made of their home. The whole world is a tragedy. Those stories are old and common."

"So, you're a do-gooder now?" *Is that hope in my voice?*

"Hardly." The wild, slightly violent light reenters his eyes. "But do you not wonder, my monster brethren, if we might get an impossible love like the musician and her dragon? Are we—mutated creations the gods never planned—allowed mates? In all my years, all my travels, my partner has never appeared to me."

The question tears at my gut as Moira's image blares in high-definition in my mind.

"You want it too, don't you?" The monster scoops up a handful of fish bones and lets them trickle through his fingers like water. "That's why I thought you would like the story. The Winged One allowed the dragon to regain his human form decades before he should have been able to. The tale shows nothing is immutable." One bone remains in his grasp, and Sev studies the sharp tip with the focus of a falcon eyeing the mouse in their talon. "The gods change their minds."

The deadly contemplation clears from his face like fog wiped from a glass.

"This has been grand, my liege." He bows deep and

straightens with a hard mask over his features. "Now, kindly fuck off."

Sev disappears through one of the wide doorways in the swirl of red robe.

"Uncomfortable, as always," I respond to the empty space where he stood.

The title he gave was all mockery. We both know who is the more powerful of the two of us. The only reasons I hold the Folk Haven Council seat is because I'm more personable and he's not interested in a political office.

Without Sev at my side, his house takes on an ominous air. I wouldn't put it past him to have set booby traps in every room. With a sweep, I gather up a handful of the fish bones and take my leave. I don't know that the sharp bones will provide any kind of evidence, but I need to have something when I tell Moira MacNamara what tried to steal her brother's selkie skin.

I step into a still-warm evening with cricket chirps filling the air, and I welcome a soft breeze that helps push the humidity around.

Despite the not-so-great news I have to deliver, I find myself smiling as I climb into my car. Tension only increases every time I interact with Moira, all set into motion from that brief kiss during the Gauntlet. Then, after the trip to the coast—where things went so well, only to implode—I was sure my hopes were useless. But the selkie's last words to me play through my head, her tone desperate rather than angry.

"You should stay away from me."

Now, I have an excuse not to.

Thank you so much for reading SUCKER FOR A SIREN. I hope you enjoyed Neri and Seamus's love story! Do you want to spend more time in the mythic-filled Folk Haven? Explore the following books for more small town, sexy, fated mates romances.

SWEARING AT A SEA MONSTER

Folk Haven Book 3

Moira MacNamara takes shit from no one, and that includes Levi Abadi, the enticing, infuriating monster who thinks he can dictate what she does with her own property. She makes a deal with him, sealed in blood. But now she can't help noticing how her veins thrum with heat every time he comes near...

SEDUCED BY A SELKIE

Folk Haven Book 1

Delta Novac hates Folk Haven, and as soon as she's done cleaning out her father's mess of a house, she's giving the town her taillights. But after she dives into the lake to save a drowning man that's not actually in danger, she finds herself with a sweet and sexy selkie shadow ready to do anything to get her to stay.

If you enjoyed SUCKER FOR A SIREN, please consider rating and reviewing the book. Reviews help other readers discover my books, which helps me make a living and funds my ability to write more mythical romances for you!

STAY IN FOLK HAVEN

You don't have to leave Folk Haven just yet! Keep reading for a sneak peek of *Swearing at a Sea Monster*, book two in the Folk Haven series...

SWEARING AT A SEA MONSTER

MOIRA

When I push through the front doors of Town Hall, I'm ready to go to battle. My territory is under attack.

Sort of. No one has shown up on the shores in Viking boats, attempting to pillage my village, or convinced me to wheel a giant wooden horse behind my protective walls.

This assault is subtler but an attack all the same.

Despite my simmering anger, I keep a professionally pleasant smile on my face as I walk through the grandest building in Folk Haven. Not that there's much competition. Tucked away in the forests of northeastern Georgia, this small town boasts few impressive buildings, tending to tilt toward quaint. But Town Hall tries to put on airs with its towering ceilings and ornate molding and polished marble floors. Wood would have suited the space fine, but the founders of Folk Haven had a point to prove.

To whom? I'm still not sure.

"Heya, Moira. Council meeting today?" The greeting comes as I pass by a cracked door.

I pause long enough to peek my head in, meeting the kind

eyes of Samantha, police chief and mermaid. That second fact makes her one of my constituents.

"It is. We're having two petitioners come to speak at nine thirty. If they accidentally wander in here, can you point them our way?"

"Will do. Do I know them?" Normally, the question would be laughable. With a town this small, it's hard not to know everyone, especially when you work in a public office.

But this meeting is odd for more than one reason.

"Not sure. Two witches from out of town. They haven't been here long. Names are Morgana and Amethyst." My eyes flit down to the meeting agenda I hastily printed this morning, immediately regretting the glance when I re-read the last-minute add-on.

"Witch names if I ever heard them." The mermaid snorts as she absentmindedly drags her fingers through inch-long blonde strands. A habit she's had since grade school, although back then, her tresses grew past her waist. I can still remember how her milk-pale skin would flush a blotchy red when our classmates called her Rapunzel. No one is brave enough to do so now that she's got a gun hooked to her belt. "I'll keep an eye out. I'm on the desk till the rest of the slackers show up."

The rest referring to the three other police officers Folk Haven has. A tiny force for a tiny town.

Not that I'm complaining.

Less police means less people to catch me after I murder Levi Abadi for sticking my business on The Council agenda.

"Thanks." I manage to keep my renewed anger out of my voice as I head farther into the building to the room reserved the first Monday of each month for the Folk Haven Mythic Council meeting.

When I push the door open and find the space empty, I silently thank my brother Seamus for grabbing me a latte this morning, so I didn't have to delay with a side trip to Coffee & Claws.

Now, I can pick a power position. One more tool in my arsenal against the coming attack. I'm debating if my back should be to the windows when Trayvon, the mayor's assistant, shuffles in, carrying a tray with water and glasses.

"You're early," he chirps, friendly smile solidly in place, even as his armful wobbles.

"Here. I can get that." I pluck the tray from his arms and carefully place the load on the conference table.

"Thank you." He uses his empty hand to push a set of curls even tighter than mine off his forehead. "I forgot there was a reason I never tried waiting tables." He grins, flashing a set of slightly-crooked-in-a-charming-way white teeth. "Do you know, I've spilled at least three drinks on Mayor Nightson, and she still hasn't fired me? People have to think I'm blackmailing her to keep my job."

If anyone thinks that, they're obtuse. Trayvon graduated with a 4.0 GPA in political science and could easily have gotten a job in a larger town or a city like Atlanta. And since he's a human, no one would have blamed him for leaving this town built primarily for mythical creatures. But he came home, and Belinda Nightson knows the importance of keeping talent in Folk Haven. She immediately took the young man under her wing. Literally and figuratively, seeing as how the woman is a griffin.

We go through the normal small talk as I settle in the best chair at the table. Trayvon's upbeat conversation abruptly ends with the next arrival.

Juan Greymark, beta of the Folk Haven wolf pack and council member representing Of the Claw mythics, meanders into the room.

Trayvon gives the shifter a tight smile, polite nod, and then beats a quick retreat. Juan and I exchange a silent look, both knowing what the other is thinking.

He's going to need to get over that if he ever wants to become mayor.

Tray's friendly nature shuts off around the wolves. Not out of fear. The exact opposite. Greymark's daughter broke the human boy's heart when she decided to go to college in Canada and stay there.

One more piece of the gossip foundation that supports a small town. I'm convinced the entirety of Folk Haven would crumble without all the little dramas that fill townsfolk's lives.

But that doesn't mean I'm going to give a slight against me a free pass.

As Juan pulls out a chair that has him facing the door, another council member arrives.

"Hello, Georgiana," I offer the greeting as I arrange my items, trying to smooth the wrinkles out of the agenda I scrunched up in anger after reading it the first time. Despite the itchy annoyance still coursing through my veins, I cannot abide the cluttered appearance. If I'm going to win the upcoming showdown, I need to be an utter professional. Not a petulant child.

Tomorrow is the dark moon, I remind myself. *I'll get to swim for the whole night in my selkie form. Slip into the cool water and finally be free from all responsibility for a time.* The thought helps me calm myself and pull on my usual unflappable boss-bitch armor.

"Moira," the siren responds with a beauty-pageant smile. The expression sits perfectly on her Southern belle face.

I never trust that kind of smile. That's the expression the senators wore before knifing Caesar in the back—I'm sure of it.

Not that I would ever call the woman on it. Georgiana is a master at twisting words to her benefit, which helped her win the council spot reserved for an Of the Wing mythic. Still, I get the sense that the majority viewpoints of her constituents are shifting from traditional to progressive, and the siren might not come out the next election with a victory. Will be interesting to watch next year.

My own council seat race was laughably easy. I would have relished a true competition. My only challenger was a merman who made promises like he was running for student body president.

Later noise curfews on the lake! First choice for fishing spots! Free boats for every voter!

That last one, which I'm sure he thought was his clincher, shot him in the fin. People knew an empty promise when they heard it, and my practice of visiting every water mythic to discuss their needs and concerns garnered me over eighty percent of the votes. Maybe next time, someone will give me an actual fight.

"I am awake before noon. I hope you all are happy." The whip of a voice comes from the doorway as the witch council member enters. Selena strolls to the first open chair and collapses into the thing like a sulky teenager rather than the sixty-year-old woman she is.

Even though Selena's views and voting practices are unpredictable, I've reached the conclusion that I like the witch. Like me, she takes no shit and is up front about the fact.

"So sorry to have disturbed your beauty rest," Georgiana offers with the exact amount of sweetener required to convey her contempt for the witch.

"Not all of us can naturally look this gorgeous. Goddess knows I can't." Selena rubs strong hands over onyx cheeks with the smoothness of a woman thirty years her junior. "Thank the elements for healing witches and their cosmetic spells. Of course, you wouldn't know anything about those, Georgiana, would you?"

The blow lands. The siren must be approaching fifty, and

she has yet to show a wrinkle in her ivory skin. With the amount of judgmental eye-squinting she does, there should at least be the hint of crow's-feet. Even at thirty-five, I'm starting to spot creases when I look in the mirror.

Georgiana doesn't say a word, but a flash of fury in her eyes, there and gone, is plenty revealing.

Seems like today has everyone on edge.

I should focus more on playing peacekeeper than revving up for my own fight. The Council is supposed to act as an example for the residents of the town. To show how mythics can coexist and work together.

We have in the past. There are even times we all unanimously agree on an issue. Rare, but it has happened. At the core, I do believe we all have the good of Folk Haven driving our decisions. The definition of *good* is what causes problems.

At one time, The Council only had to deal with four differing views. In those days, the mayor acted as a deciding vote in the event of a tie. But in the original bylaws, The Council creators stated a new seat could be added if a faction of forty or more mythics, gathered under a similar grouping, petitioned for a space. Hence the addition made a year ago.

Monsters—aka today's pain in my ass.

As if summoned by my silent seething, the door opens one final time to reveal my nemesis.

Levi Abadi.

Keep reading Swearing at a Sea Monster...

AUTHOR'S NOTE

At the end of 2020, I moved to northern Georgia, an area full of gorgeous lakes. Within weeks, the beginning of a story formed in my mind. I couldn't let go of the idea of a selkie family living in a lake cove, trying to find a safe place for themselves in this ever-changing world.

Then, I read a news article one day about an unfortunate accident where a man had drowned in a lake not too far from my home. One message in the report stood out to me: deaths on lakes were inevitable; however, this lake in particular experienced a higher rate than any other, and the large number had no clear explanation.

My mind caught on that fact. Morbid, I know. But I couldn't let it go. Why would a lake have a higher mortality rate? With my selkie story already germinating, the idea of evil magic immediately rose in response. And so the story of The Collector formed, as did the history of Lake Galen.

Lake Galen is an entirely fictional lake, inspired by many bodies of water in both Georgia and South Carolina. But as I researched, I found that the sad story I'd made up for the creation of Folk Haven held similarities to the lake previously discussed in that news article.

Lake Linear.

Lake Lanier, I learned, covers a painful marker of one of our country's many mistreatments of Black residents. The former town of Oscarville—a historically Black town—sits, abandoned, at the bottom of Lake Lanier, not because the townspeople were asked to leave and given fair compensation for relocation, but because, in 1912, a white mob eradicated almost the whole population.

My Folk Haven series is *not* a rewriting or retelling of the violent history of Lake Lanier. But I cannot ignore the similarities between a real lake covering up the history of a Black town destroyed by racial injustice and my fake lake covering up land sowed with twisted magic by an evil man.

That is why I encourage my readers to take a moment to learn about Oscarville and the other drowned towns in the United States. Amber Ruffin provides a poignant summary on the topic in an episode of The Amber Ruffin Show. Also, consider donating to organizations like Facing History & Ourselves.

And thank you for reading my story!

NEWSLETTER SIGN UP

Get another Folk Haven romance for FREE! Sign up for my newsletter to receive *A Selkie's Secret,* a novella that tells the story of Isla, a selkie, and Finn, the human she refuses to fall in love with...

ALSO BY LAUREN CONNOLLY

Paranormal

Folk Haven

A Selkie's Secret (Book 0.5)

Seduced by a Selkie (Book 1)

Sucker for a Siren (Book 2)

Swearing at a Sea Monster (Book 3) – coming January 2022

Casual Magic

Fire Magic & Ice Cream (Book 1) – coming spring 2022

Seasonal Magic

Remembering a Witch (Book 1)

Wanting a Witch (Book 2)

Contemporary

Forget the Past

Rescue Me (Book 1)

Read Me (Book 2)

Resist Me (Book 3) – coming soon

Standalone Novel

You Only Need One

ABOUT THE AUTHOR

Lauren Connolly is a Colorado Book Awards Finalist and an author of contemporary and paranormal romance stories. She's lived among mountains, next to lakes, and in imaginary worlds. Lauren can never seem to stay in one place for too long, but trust that wherever she's residing there is a dog who thinks he's a troll, twin cats hiding in the couch, and bookshelves bursting with the diverse stories written by the authors she loves.

www.ingramcontent.com/pod-product-compliance
Lightning Source LLC
Chambersburg PA
CBHW060926190726
48286CB00002B/653